Missing Remnants

Detective Track
Volume 1

DJ COOPER

First published by DJ Cooper, 2018

This is a work of fiction. Similarities to real people, places, or events are entirely coincidental.

MISSING REMNANTS
First edition. 14th May 2018.
This edition published in 2019 by DJsWorld Press
Copyright © 2018 DJ Cooper.
Written by DJ Cooper.

ISBN 978-1-9160713-0-8

1
The End

Headquarters buzzed with the voices of my colleagues. I heard a dirge rather than distinct voices in what, that day, struck me as an uncomfortable, dingy, oppressive place of work. An image flashed into my mind. The picture of two smiling men on a mountainside and the last time I had spent any time off the space station with my husband Jarner. He died shortly afterwards. I sighed and pushed the mental image away. Too painful, too annoying, too…

"Bunch of arse," I muttered. I know that doesn't make sense. It's my phrase and I like it. When you consider most things in life to be a bunch of arse, you realise you need a holiday. Or a career change. Or, at least the opportunity to stab that annoying little pissant through the eye with a fork. Too far? I had reached that point, so fire me.

I had a feeling that day was the day I'd find out I'd thrown too many insults and slammed my hand on too many tables. I wouldn't lash out unless provoked. The Si-Cross Four Authority did not know that. They didn't trust me, and I had a licence to wield weaponry from a separate Authority they couldn't challenge.

I'd tuned out most of the chatter behind me as I concentrated on system reports. I was ahead. It put me in uncharted territory. The summons came after lunch. Si-Cross Four is a large off-world space station boasting many places to eat. It didn't matter which I chose, I always found a small group of people who required off-menu items. They couldn't all have allergies to the latest food considered the devil's work. I was five minutes late back. And that was only because I'd stopped to help clear an area resulting in the initiation of a chemical spill false alarm report.

"Detective Trackneathan, my office," my commanding officer Beynard issued in the tone of voice you did not ignore. Not unless you wanted them removed with a rusty knife and handed to you on a platter. I logged off and pushed myself out of my chair. The chip in my knee holding the joint together dug in and I winced. Yeah, I was on a list for a permanent fix. It came with the caveat I shouldn't hold my breath.

Eyes followed me from my desk to Beynard's lair. He was a tall, thin, health freak of a man. I was shorter and more muscular but with a fitness regime hampered by my knee. I could still take him if I'd wanted to.

"Detective Trackneathan, sit." I sat. To my credit, I did not bark. I hated my name. Where the hell had Trackneathan come from? It gave rise to the joke *why Track Neathan, Neathan isn't lost.* I fidgeted. I hated the discomfort of the Authority chairs. I hated everything.

"Sit still." I may not have barked, but Beynard did. I resisted the urge to say, *What are you, my mother?* in my inimitable way of making things worse.

"You have unused leave. Take it."

I was temporarily incapable of speech. Beynard was not known for a soft side. He was as much a people person as I was. It wasn't the order that shocked me. It was the uncontrollable fear of what the hell I'd do with that much free time.

"You've accrued three months. This is beyond the limit allowed to accumulate on the system," he sat in his chair looking down at me with disdain. His lips were permanently stuck in a disapproving expression.

"OK, well, what if I carry on working and lose the leave?" I asked.

"Not an option. You either take the leave or you'll be Centred. You've been classified for study."

Despite the horror, I was not surprised. No-one wanted to be Centred. People left the station rather than spend any time at the Centre. It was a limbo of banal, meaningless tasks supervised by scientists sent to study and correct the behaviour of potential troublemakers. In my case, drop the word 'potential.'

"There has to be a way out of this? What if I work shorter shifts? Use some leave that way?

"Not an option," Beynard repeated, "You've been assessed for a while. Your attitude is deemed unacceptable. You need to hand in your Authority accreditation. I can't take your weapon, despite you and it being a risk to others."

"I am not a risk to others," I objected.

"Tell that to Byrod. He's on the list for a new jaw."

"I barely touched him. And you saw the footage. He came at me with a knife and I had to defend myself. The damn thief has had a glass jaw for years."

"Yes, but we are over our quota of allowable injuries to criminals this month. So, you put yourself in the view of the Centre with that punch. A new jaw costs money."

"Then use my leave to pay for it and I'll carry on working."

"It won't cover it."

I breathed in deeply and let out an exasperated sigh. I was running out of ideas. If my leave wasn't enough to cover the cost of a new jaw, my savings certainly weren't. The cost of medical care had never been higher for those of us with Authority Four credit. "So, what is the Authority's real view on this?" I asked, "I should have taken the knife wound and let him get away with the serum?" I stared at Beynard and scratched the side of my face. I knew the answer.

"Yes. A knife wound in you would cost the Authority less to fix than rebuilding a criminal's jaw."

My hand moved to scratch the stubble on my chin. I'd shaved that morning too. "Or maybe I should have just shot him and only accrued the cost of recycling the body," see what I mean about making trouble? Sometimes I just don't know when to stop.

"Even that would have been preferable to the cost of a new jaw," Beynard droned, as he leant on his desk and steepled his fingertips.

"You have got to be fucking kidding me," I said under my breath. I regretted my words before they left my lips. Beynard's hand shot across his desk and grabbed the swear-jar. The mug-sized, solid object lit up at his touch. Rings of green illumination began to ascend from the bottom displaying the progress of the current scheme we were collecting for.

"Can I pay with my excess leave?" I asked, knowing I wouldn't get an answer. I pressed my thumb against the jar to authorise my monetary contribution to whatever we were collecting for this month. *The true cost of fucking in the office*, I mused to myself. Whatever the cause was, I was single-handedly funding it.

I sat for a few seconds. My brain alternated between various 'what ifs' the Authority wouldn't go for, and an utter void of uselessness. "Can I transfer to a different Authority?"

"No, you have been deemed unfit for duty. You are not to act for the Si-Cross Four Authority or any other Authority in any way for the next three months. Go down to the Career Op Centre and take a course."

The idea of straddling the COC for three months failed to fill me with pleasure. I lost my train of thought for a second over that sentence but dragged myself back to reality. The last time I looked, the COC was all painting and pot making. Not the type you smoked. I had nothing against artistic things, but they weren't pastimes that filled me with excitement. I liked chasing the bad guy. Or, you know, hobbling after him. Thinking of my knee as I absently rubbed it, I asked, "Is there any news on my new knee?"

The look of surprise on Beynard's face gave me the answer before he spoke. "No. You put that on the back burner when you broke Byrod's face."

"F…." I said as a gleeful look fell over Beynard's face and he reached for the swear-jar again. I closed my mouth and savoured his look of disappointment. The jar remained on the desk, its internal light system dimmed as it fell into standby.

"Am I contributing to your retirement with this fund?" I asked.

The glare on his face! He narrowed his eyes at me. "Might I remind you accusations of defrauding the Authority must be backed up by evidence?"

The ice in his voice chipped something off my spine. "It was a joke," I said lamely.

"I suggest you go, before you get yourself into any more trouble. Clear your desk of belongings, it'll be reused by your replacement tomorrow."

And that was it. Almost twenty years working for the Authority on various stations. I'd worked my way up to detective from the bottom of nowhere. People knew me and respected me even if they didn't like me. And now I was on the way out. This was the worst one yet. This went beyond the reprimand. With one broken jaw I'd managed to circumvent the three strikes rule and head straight for the exit. Hardly anyone came back from an 'unfit for duty' tag.

The result of my meeting must have been plastered all over my face as I left Beynard's office and headed back to my desk. The kid with the floppy hair whose name always escaped me scuttled towards me. He wittered words probably to ask if I was OK. I raised a hand for silence. I wasn't listening. I wasn't in the mood.

I slumped in my chair and felt suddenly very tired. Maybe I should take a break. *And do what?* I yelled in my head and I thumped my hand down on my desk. The kid hadn't taken the hint, and he jumped out of his skin.

"What do you want?" I snapped and opened a drawer. The bag I dragged out dislodged various office paraphernalia onto the floor. The kid scrambled to retrieve them. Amongst my belongings was the picture frame I used to keep on my desk until the memories became too painful.

"Is this?" the kid didn't finish his sentence. I reached for the antique frame and gazed at the couple in the picture. It felt a lifetime ago.

"Jarner, my husband. Decorated war hero. Died in the conflict. Yeah, that's him."

"Shit, I'm sorry. I didn't know."

I was touched. How stupid is that? I was touched by the fact the kid would risk any of his minuscule pay on the swear-jar over me. I looked up at him as I put the frame in my bag and saw just how young they were recruiting them these days.

"What's your name again?" I asked, for the sixth time since he'd arrived.

"Laiten, Sir." There was feeling in his eyes if I'd interpreted anything right. I almost cracked a smile.

"There's never been any reason for you to call me 'Sir'. It's Detective officially, but mostly Track. People who are tired of living call me Trackneathan." I regretted the unwarranted threat as I dumped more personal tat into my bag and corrected myself. "From this point onwards, as I've been relieved of duty for ninety days, there's no point in you calling me anything. My replacement will be here in the morning." I had to hand it to him, either this kid was a damn fine actor, or he was truly disappointed at the news.

"I was looking forward to working with you S… Track," his voice was quiet.

"Well, I'm sure there are better people to guide you through an Authority career, Laiten. Much better people than me." I zipped up my bag and gave my surroundings a brief visual. I was sure my successor would forward on anything I'd left behind. The chances of me leaving the station were slim. I had the finances, I just couldn't be bothered.

As I turned I saw a small farewell party behind me. "Who won the pool?" I asked of a silent room. "Oh, come on, someone must have started a book on when they finally ousted me from this gig. Who won?"

They turned to look at Wicklow. Fiercely intelligent, could think on her feet, excellent undercover. Even I could see she was an attractive brunette. I'd partnered her, she'd never failed to get the heart of a target racing. I'd miss working with her. I would miss her friendship. She briefly closed her eyes and shook her head once and said, "Hegland."

"Bastard," I replied. My drinking partner, and after Jarner, my best friend. And probably the most qualified to predict when I'd go too far. Wicklow rushed forward and threw her arms around my broad shoulders. She knew I was joking when I said, "Don't go getting soft on me Wick. It's about time you learnt to stand on your own two feet."

She pulled away and slapped my arm and said, "Like I haven't been carrying you all this time."

I nodded. She'd pulled me out of a jam many times over the years.

A siren sounded throughout the rooms and the team scrambled to ready themselves for whatever was coming their way. I looked over to Beynard who had spent the last few minutes standing in his doorway, no doubt making sure I left the area. He stared at me and raised his arm. His finger pointed towards the exit as he mouthed the letters "C.O.C."

2
Ethan's Ol' Bar

I turned my back on Si-Cross Four's Authority HQ and left my colleagues to the chaos. I needed a drink. Hegland was still undercover. When it came down to it, I didn't have that many friends. Either, they couldn't tolerate me, or I couldn't be bothered with them. I was a Positive Mental Attitude Guru's worst nightmare or biggest challenge.

I'd left the strap too long and the body of the bag knocked into my right knee as I walked. I was going to need alcohol just to take the pain away. Pitiful excuse. Nevertheless, I stopped off at the recreation level and headed into Ethan's Ol' Bar. There had never been an Ethan, only someone trying to be clever with the word ethanol. I'd given the moniker to the resident service robot, and it had stuck. His real designation was Delta 172. I preferred Ethan and he never objected.

"Are you not working the crisis, Track?"

"Nah Ethan, I've been grounded."

"That's a shame, Track. What would you like?"

"Rum, mix it," he knew what I meant. You programmed your preferences into the system and your drink never varied. I scanned my thumb for payment and thanked the robot for my drink. I had never been clear on the protocol, but manners cost nothing. I might have been an intolerable arse of a man, but I tried not to be rude. To cut any further small talk short with my metal composite companion, I took my drink to my corner table. I'd glared at people who dared to sit at that table enough times for most of the regulars to avoid it. If I hadn't been so security conscious I'd have sat with my back to the world and faced the corner. I believe the term is 'miserable git'. I have my moments.

The place was deserted. The atmosphere was *late night* at all times of the space station's day. I spotted one other person in a corner shrouded in shadow. I couldn't tell if it was anyone I knew. Successfully avoiding eye-contact, I started making mental lists. If I had been benched for three months, I had to come up with a plan. With no roadmap, I saw me in my apartment in my food-stained underwear with a beard down to my chest and a variety of snack products stuck in my hair. I knew I was a cliché, but I had no intention of becoming *that* cliché.

My thoughts turned to the COC and available courses. If the hierarchy had more tolerance for me, I could have reached headier heights than detective by now. I liked the work I did. I had little interest in doing anything else.

I wasn't into pottery, embroidery, painting or drawing and had no aptitude or interest for those things. I couldn't and didn't want to play a musical instrument, and I'd been told in no uncertain terms by my late husband that I was tone deaf.

We had the usual range of self-help courses on the station that I had little enthusiasm for. I liked who I was and didn't want to change—even if I was a bastard to get along with. I wasn't a fan of people telling me how to think. I liked my own thoughts.

We had sports teams. I didn't do people and didn't do sport. I did detecting and… my train of thought was interrupted by a clang from the bar. I looked up to see Ethan's mechanical, almost human looking head shoot up and judder to the side. He stared down at the space where until a few seconds ago, his right arm had been attached.

"Hang on, Ethan," I said as I grabbed my glass from the table and my bag from the floor and made my way over to my non-human buddy. I downed the dregs of my rum, dropped my bag and reached into my back pocket of my trousers for my multi-tool. I opened the hatch to the back of the bar and silenced the alarm before it reached its ear-splitting level. It had a tone that made me want to throttle someone. Most things did these days.

Ethan's arm was dead on the floor. I scrabbled around looking for the attachment pin. The robots possessed a strange characteristic similar to human shock when bits of them fell off. Ethan was frozen to the spot. He came to slightly as I stood bearing both the arm and the attachment pin.

"Thank you, Track," he said. I shook my head,

"I haven't fixed you yet," I said as I frowned. "This isn't the correct pin for your arm. I'll have a look in my workshop and see if I've got a replacement." My workshop was a glorified desk just inside my front door. On it, I had all the miscellaneous mechanical parts I'd picked up over the years. I put pictures on the system announcing the parts I'd found and offered my services to reattach or return them. I was quite handy with various mechanical things. Not so hot with circuitry. I had a few success stories. By and large, the various parts remained unclaimed.

The station had a biological event a few years back. The true cause was never made public, but we suspected someone dropped a contagion near a vent and the quarantine procedures didn't trigger before it got out. Amputations to stop the spread of the resulting infection saved the lives of those it didn't kill. The Authorities were responsible and had to stump up the cost-pardon the pun-for the treatment and initial prosthetics issued to the survivors. Of course, the Authority was not liable for any ongoing costs. I helped out where I could, just because I could. It made me feel better about being a bastard to contend with the rest of the time.

"There," I said, "It'll hold for a bit. If I have one, I'll bring in a better pin later and have another go."

"Thank you, Track," Ethan replied, in his clipped robotic tone. He tested his arm. It was adequate. "Would you like another drink? This one would be on the house because you performed a service beyond your usual tasks."

"That's not why I did it, but sure, why not? Thanks."

Dark liquid sloshed onto the bar as I disengaged the alarm and took up residence on the patron's side. Ethan's arm was not performing at optimum levels. The Authority didn't care. I'd discovered, like most things, Ethan was on a waiting list. for a professional service. It was surprising no-one had stepped in to pick up the contract since the service company was wiped out. It operated with a few exhausted individuals barely being paid. If I had the knowledge, I could make a killing if the Authority had the ability to pay me.

We didn't earn money anymore. We earned credit for the services we required to sustain life. You turned up and did your job and they fed you what they had. We had apartment space due to the demise of so many and the exodus of others. We were low on personnel, but high on what the Authority called 'freeloaders' amongst other choice phrases. We were remnants of a once thriving community. A few of us questioned why we were still on the station and not elsewhere. We were a halfway point between bigger and better places. Bigger to the left and better to the right! Occasionally, more important people than us stopped off to use our facilities, only to sanitise their hands on their way out. They added to our economy, so we did our best to accommodate them whilst hiding the seedier, more decrepit side of our existence from them.

I heard the noise behind me before my brain had registered what it was.

"Detective Track, I need your help."

I recognised her. The woman was young but the scarring and lines on her face made her look much older than her twenty-something years. I didn't know her personally. I just recognised her from around the station.

"I'm sorry, I'm not working as a detective at the moment. Anything Authority related should be reported directly to the desk." I paused, "Unless it's your leg?" Maybe I shouldn't have mentioned her prosthesis, some considered it a failure of etiquette. Despite no qualifications, it happened to be the only thing I could help with at that time.

She swayed in the dim light of the bar and I reached out to catch her. She righted herself and took a step backwards. "Are you not with the Authority anymore?"

In the light, I couldn't tell what the expression was on her face. Her voice sounded small and childlike as if I'd shattered her life. I regretted having to dismiss her, but I had no choice. "Not for the next three months, I'm afraid. You need to lodge any crimes and complaints at the desk. For the next ninety days, I have been returned to civilian status. I have as much access to the system as you do." Civilian access meant you could see if anyone had been assigned your issue and the status it had. 'Pending' meant it hadn't been picked up yet. 'Ongoing' was obvious, 'Closed' could mean anything from we have resolved your issues, and everyone accepts the outcome to we closed it because we don't have the resources to take it any further. Unless there was a major escalation, cases were rarely re-opened. That said, crime on the station was not rife. Or that was what I assumed. And we all know what they say about assuming things. "Honestly," I said, "go to the desk and give them the details. They'll be able to help."

She was far from happy with my efforts but said no more. She hung her head, and I watched as she took a few faltering steps away from me.

Again, with my big mouth, "If you need me to look at your leg, you'll find me on the map." Some people did not want to be reminded of their artificial limbs, every day was a reminder. She nodded once and limped away.

As the conversation between two humans had ended, Ethan stepped out of the shadows. "Would you like another drink, Track?"

"No, thank you, Ethan, I'd better get back and feed Banyon," I said as I finished the last drop and stood.

"Goodbye Track."

"See ya later Eth," I said as I shouldered my bag and I too limped out of the bar.

After a few steps, my joints remembered how to work again, and my movement became more fluid. I wasn't winning races anytime soon, but I was still able to get about with my knee in the state it was.

Up and down were not desired activities, so I took the lift to my apartment. The hall lights flickered which was only disconcerting because I was old enough to remember the life-support failure years before. Despite flickering lights being the norm on the habitat floors, they had preceded the failure. I'd been wary ever since.

I opted for key card entry. It was currently the most reliable system. The door to my apartment slid open and Banyon raced to the door yapping loudly and waggling his ears and tail. "Banyon, here boy, quickly." Yes, I was pleased to see him. I was more concerned he'd slipped his silent mode again. "Quick, before we get another complaint lodged by our friendly neighbours," I said as I pulled back the fake fur and reset Banyon to silent.

We were allowed replica pets in the apartment, providing they didn't cause any trouble to the neighbours. I missed the deaf old man I'd had living next to me six months ago. This new couple had lodged two noise complaints against me since they'd moved in five and a half months ago. Out of all the spare apartments at their disposal Mr and Mrs 'no we don't care about your family heirloom replica dog' had chosen something next to me.

I think I mentioned I don't do people. Neither did the old man. We got on well. Whenever he needed his legs adjusted, he'd remove one of them and bang it on the wall. Fine, when I was home. I'd take my toolkit, reattach it and off he'd go. Not so great when I was at work. The old duffer had no concept of time and bashed a dent in his wall for hours until I'd made it home and round to his place. So many conversations of, "How many hours have you been banging on the wall today?"

"Meh, not many."

I'd give him a disapproving look. But what did I care? I wasn't there to hear it.

I was just finishing fussing over Banyon's fake ears when my doorbell sounded. Today's chime of choice was an ancient pig sound. "Go to your bed, let me deal with this," I opened the door about to apologise for the yapping. The woman from earlier in the bar fell through the doorway. She died, just like someone had hit her off switch.

3
Interference

It was probably because this had never happened in my home that I hesitated. At work, I'd have leapt or limped into action. I could hear a quiet mewling from Banyon in his basket in the corner. Old robotic personalities were a dying art form. But not as dead as the woman in the doorway of my apartment. After a few seconds, I tore my gaze away from her and pulled my comms unit out of my pocket. The battery system that never degrades was dead.

I went old-school and hit a button on the wall. I'd never got the hang of implanted technology and kept calling the wrong people or leaving the call open. I had endured so many 'old man' labels as a result.

"Authority Four."

"Get me Wicklow, it's Track." There was a pause.

"She's busy."

"Tell her I need to take her out on a date." Another pause. It was our 'I'm in trouble' code phrase from long ago. It had been assigned to us shortly after everyone found out I was gay. It did the trick. Her voice was rushed,

"Track, we're right in the middle of something. Can it wait?"

"No, I need you at my apartment, ASAP."

"Not going to be possible. Unless this is a matter of life and death…"

I cut her off, "There's a dead woman in my apartment."

There were a few seconds of silence before, "I'll be right over."

The comms link went dead. I checked the time. Whatever they were dealing with when I left that afternoon I wasn't expecting any movement for at least half an hour.

"What the hell is going on here?"

Why does that happen? Why do your nosy, interfering, meddlesome neighbours always turn up at your door the moment you have a dead woman obstructing your threshold? I thought about saying, 'move along here, there's nothing to see,' but I was a miserable bastard, not a liar.

"The team are on their way. Have you just arrived home?"

"Yes. What did you do to her?"

My jaw dropped and for a second, I was speechless. Miserable bastard, yes, bloody murderer, no. I gave them a stern look. I'm not sure they noticed the difference. He was giving me some alpha male bravado which fell flat. She was bending over the body about to touch it.

"Step away from the body. Do not interfere with the crime scene."

"How do we know you haven't?" he asked.

What can I say? You always find some arse somewhere who thinks he knows everything including your job. "Please go back to your apartment and stay there until the detectives arrive to take statements."

"Why don't you do that?" he asked as she straightened up, refusing to take her eyes off the prosthetic leg. I noted neither of them had prosthetic limbs and assumed it was morbid curiosity on her part.

"I am a witness. I can't conduct any interviews," I said.

"You might be the murderer for all we know," him again.

I sighed, "If I'd had anything to do with her death, I'd have pulled her body through the door and locked us in," I replied. The truth was, I was beginning to wonder if I did have something to do with her death. She'd sought me out earlier for some reason and I'd turned her away. Now this.

"Well I think you're perfectly capable of committing the crime," he said.

I heard Banyon growl in the background. His silent mode was slipping again. I needed to upgrade his control system.

"And that dog of yours is a nuisance and should be destroyed," he pointed his finger at Banyon.

"Banyon is a family heirloom replica. As such, his existence is protected by Authority Ruling Eighty-Eight, Subsection Sixteen," OK, miserable bastard and a liar. So, arrest me- there was no such ruling. No-one interfered with Banyon. "Banyon has broken no rules," I said, "I have broken no rules by keeping him."

"He's noisy," she interrupted.

"So are you when you're having sex," I replied. I'd slipped into unprofessional mode. Sometimes I couldn't stop my mouth. I'd never heard them have sex.

He put his arm around her and ushered her towards their apartment. "You'll hear more about this," he threatened.

"No doubt," I replied.

After they had left, I stood over… I didn't even know her name and I knew better than to search her bag and pockets for ID. The less I had to do with her, the better. The one thing I'd learnt about this existence was you had to look after yourself because no-one else gave a damn. I'd be accused of her murder if they so much as found a trace of me on her. The best I could do for me and the young woman was to stand back, not contaminate the scene and therefore not divert the investigation away from its correct path.

I took my own pictures. An act of self-preservation- in case I was accused in some way. I noted her left prosthetic leg. It was one of the earlier models. The silver and blue metal construction was scratched. There had been no attempt to colour the limbs to match skin tone. Many people used artificial limbs not even made for them. It was a life of pain and sores.

Her skirt reached above her knees. I noticed some

bruising on her thighs and bare arms. This wasn't unusual for the survivors of the biological incident. As well as needing limbs amputated, they were left with lifelong issues of fatigue, coordination problems and pains in muscles and joints. They stumbled into things and injured themselves on a regular basis. The wealthy could afford assistance. By and large the wealthy had left Si-Cross Four.

Her top was a uniform combination I knew I should recognise. For the life of me, I couldn't pull the name of her employer out of my brain. She didn't work at a place I frequented often which ruled out my local food supplier, the bar and Authority Four. What a dull life! I should probably get out more.

Her medium dark hair had been ravished by the illness. It had the usual brittle and translucent look to it. Underneath the artificial nail coverings, I was sure her fingernails would be tinged with grey like every other survivor's.

I noticed something I should have seen the moment she collapsed at my door. She was missing her shoe. I didn't know if this was important but was annoyed I'd paid her little attention earlier in Ethan's. Not that I usually notice the shoes women wear, but I was supposed to be observant.

I heard the lift arrive at the end of my corridor and readied myself for the onslaught of questions.

The sounds of swishing material preceded personnel dressed in biohazard suits. I was about to protest until I realised I'd made the assumption of murder and the team had made one of outbreak. At this stage, either was a possibility. So much for protecting my neighbours! I took a step backwards until it occurred to me I'd been in the vicinity of a possible pathogen for the last few minutes.

I heard Wicklow's voice before I connected it to the masked individual standing in front of me. She stepped to the side as the retrieval team bagged the young woman's body.

"Let's go inside and you can fill me in," she instructed.

Habit made me push the door shut behind me.

"Leave it open," she said.

Banyon had not made the connection between the voice and our friend and he remained in his basket. His ears occasionally flicked, and his tail continued to swish exactly every three seconds.

"Is the suit necessary?" I asked.

"We don't know yet," Wicklow replied.

I told her the details of my afternoon from leaving HQ, to talking to the woman at Ethan's and the conversation with my neighbours. I probably should have mentioned that first,

"Go next door and secure the neighbours, they've potentially been exposed," Wicklow called to someone made anonymous by their suit. I heard a scream from the woman next door and a loud protest from him as the team entered their home.

"At least they get the new decontamination pods, they won't feel a thing," I was beginning to sulk.

"Was she displaying any symptoms when you spoke to her earlier?" Wicklow asked. I thought for a moment.

"Nothing like the last outbreak, no. All the long-term side effects of having survived the outbreak, but nothing else."

"How well did you know her?" Wicklow asked. She had already asked me twice. I knew what she was doing. Ask the same question differently several times to try to catch the interviewee out.

"As I said, I recognise her, but I don't know where from. She doesn't work in food, or the bar or Authority Four. I've probably just seen her around. Come on Wick, is this necessary? You know me. Why the hell would I want to kill anyone? It's too much effort."

"You're missing the point. You still think this is murder. We're still operating under the assumption it's an outbreak of some kind. As such, we don't know what if anything may be contaminated. We have a major delegation coming in soon. You know the drill. We have to make sure Si-Cross Four is clean and clear from any contamination before they arrive. We have to lock down all the undesirable areas and seal them off from prying eyes. And we need to keep all but the essential Remnants out of sight."

"Are we ever going to stop using the term *Remnants*?" I was suddenly fuming. "It's hideous. They are still people. They did not seek to be contaminated, they would not have chosen to have their limbs amputated if there had been any other way for them to survive. Calling them Remnants is fucking awful Wick, and I expected better from you. It could have happened to anyone. Me, you, your husband. Would you use the term if it was one of us?" My disappointment in my friend's use of the word was etched on my face. I looked at her with disgust. I had never liked the word when the designation was first used when we saw the outbreak was survivable. It was an official term and one I wholeheartedly and very vocally objected to. I could see Wicklow tilt her head slightly forward.

"I'm sorry, Track. I'm exhausted. And I'm shit scared of another outbreak. You might as well know. I'm pregnant. Remember I had a mild form of the virus, contamination, whatever the hell it was. What if my baby is affected because I was? What if it's passed down now because it's in me? I know that's not an excuse. I hate the term too."

I had no answers for her. I wanted to congratulate her. But the track record on pregnancies wasn't brilliant. I wanted to console her, but she was in the damn suit. And it was probably the best place for her if this was a contamination of some kind. I remained unconvinced. I had no evidence, but I had a gut feeling this wasn't a biological event or an accident. Deep down I knew the young woman was murdered. But I was off the job. I had no means to investigate and in my current status, I had no input. HQ would effectively be turning its back on me for the next three months.

I heard protests from outside. Through the open door, I saw what I assumed to be my neighbours in bio-suits being manhandled towards the service lifts at the other end of the corridor. Another member of HQ entered my apartment holding a spare suit.

"No, oh come on Wick. You know with the chip in my knee I have to go through the old decontamination process. It's burning hot water and wire brushes. Do you really need to put me through that?"

4
Flayed

The journey to decontamination did not take long enough. A year wouldn't have been long enough. I hated the pain of the brushes. I hated the scraped skin and the inevitable bleeding from somewhere. This would be my third time. And I rued the day I took the option for the chip in my knee. It did its job, but it couldn't be put near any of the new decontamination units or it would fail and cause more damage to what was left of the joint. Knowing the complications people suffered from the prosthetics, I was determined to keep all my limbs if at all possible.

I didn't make it difficult for Wicklow. She was only following procedure. Plus, she was pregnant. Despite everything that was going on at that moment I was happy for her. They had been discussing a family for years. Most couples decided against the option. The heartache of multiple failed pregnancies was too much to bear.

"Are you pleased?" I asked, aware any conversation we had in the suits was automatically recorded for the Authority. She turned her body so she could look at me. I could just about make out her face in the helmet. Her expression was unreadable.

"It wasn't planned," was her only reply. I got the feeling she needed to tell me more as a friend, not a colleague. We'd had that kind of relationship. She could talk to me with the assurance I would never try to get her into bed. Surprisingly, given the correct amount of rum, I was a good listener. I also didn't gossip. Admittedly, a lot of the time that was because I'd forgotten what someone had told me. But really, I just couldn't be bothered.

"I wish there was another way," Wicklow said, "I know you were in a bad state last time you went through this."

"Two weeks," I began, "Two weeks I was in bed with skin infections they could barely control. I was supposed to be decontaminated. Instead, they laid me open to a shit load of infection."

"They have improved the system now. I checked it out earlier when the initial panic from the alarm had died down,"

I interrupted her, "What was that about?" I asked as a long shot. Sure enough,

"You know I can't tell you, you were benched before it happened. What I was saying was, I checked out the improvements to the old-fashioned decontamination system. I'm pregnant, if anything gets out, I won't be able to use the pods either. They have better infection control for the old system now. I checked the inventory and all the necessary drugs are already on the station. There won't be the delay there was last time in treating any side effects."

"Can the drugs be used on you if you're pregnant?" I asked. I was deflecting. Cruel, I know, but I'd rather think of someone else potentially going through the old decon system than the certainty it was in *my* immediate future.

"I'm not sure. But at least the old system won't damage the baby."

The lift stopped. I blew out a deep breath. I tried to move my hands to wipe them over my face. All I managed to do was smear the front of the helmet I was now wearing.

We exited the lift, bumping into each other as neither of us took into account our extra width from the suits. The old decontamination suite was behind a grey door set back in a grey wall. The corridor was dimly lit to save power. The area thankfully wasn't in high demand. I looked at Wicklow and she returned my look as she entered through one door for suit decontamination. She would merely be sprayed. I entered through the other door for my own personal flaying session.

As the door opened, I held the unlikely hope the personnel required to remove several layers of skin were not present. I might as well have hoped for the resurrection of my late husband. I missed him in times like these. Jarner had a smile that didn't light up the room, it was too small for that. It was a private smile just for the two of us. A slight upturn of his lips, but a brightness to his eyes that would lift any bad mood I found myself in. He also wouldn't have let me procrastinate. He would have placed a boot on my arse and kicked me into the decon area and told me to "Get on with it Track, I didn't marry you for you to become a sodding wimp."

I sighed. I missed him.

I knew the drill. I removed my suit in the first room and placed it in the receptacle. They'd clean it up and reuse it. My own clothes, had I been wearing them, would likely have been incinerated due to the difference in fabric. I was idly grateful I hadn't changed out of my HQ uniform. They could do what they liked with the damn thing. Knowing my luck, the uniforms would respond to decon and they'd appear back in the system for me to collect, providing they ever let me back into HQ.

I stared blindly at the sign on the wall above the suit shoot. The bio suit was already winging its way to its own decon adventure. I wished I was it and not me.

Out of the corner of my eye, I could see the techs take a step towards the glass wall to determine why I was delaying. I waved them off. I removed and threw my shoes into the boot box. I nearly ripped my uniform from my body in an attempt to get this physical torture over with. This pain would be nothing close to the pain of losing Jarner. I had to focus on that fact. The uniform disappeared into the corresponding shoot. This prompted the door to the decontamination chamber to open. I walked into the room.

The water jets started up. The temperature was adjusted. It was a mixture of water and cleansing chemical to break down any known contaminants we'd experienced on the base. It wasn't enough to soak in the shower. The two sadists who were probably decent people trying to earn enough food to feed their families approached, protected by more suits.

"Ready?" the taller one asked. I wanted to scream 'no' and run to the door. The memory of Jarner kept me there. He expected better of me. He expected me to tough it out. I nodded and closed my eyes. The first application of the brush on my chest took my breath away. The pain felt like the tips of many knives scraping down my torso. And this was just how it felt on my chest. There were far worse areas they'd eventually get to. I did my best to block everything out. I knew from reading about it how long the experience lasted. I never had a concept of time while I was going through it.

I started out tough enough. Standing, battered, scorched and determined to last longer than I did the last time. At some point, I must have done the usual collapse onto the wet floor trying to protect sensitive skin whilst clasps raised from holes in the floor to pin my arms and legs down so the techs could scrub every inch of me. Before I passed out, I wondered why they couldn't hand out sedation or any form of anaesthetic before ripping me a new one.

***

Indistinct mumbling. I tightened my closed eyes against the light that was in them. It went dark. It went light. Someone groaned. I think it was me.

"Har nong gut mah?" I said.

"What did he say?"

"Beats me."

"Haw ong as nut?" I tried again.

"Do you think he's OK?"

"Give him a minute. You wanna try that again for us? Track? Can you hear me?"

"How long wasIout?" I managed two of the words before I ran the rest into each other.

"About ninety minutes," the decon tech replied.

Ugh, Jarner would be so proud. I tried to sit up. I was restrained. I wanted to yell the words 'is this really necessary' but I conserved energy instead.

"I'll release these providing you don't hit out," the other tech replied. I nodded. Evidently, it had not been a calm recovery. I could see them now. Like everyone I saw, they were young. Twenties. No, looking closer, one of them was older. My eyes were still adjusting.

"Did you get it all?" I asked turning my wrists as they were released.

"There is no sign of contaminants on your body."

"Were there signs before?" I asked. So help me if I'd just gone through that for no reason I would rip someone else a new one.

"We only test you after you finish decontamination," the older one replied. "You'll have to check with the Authority to see if there was a contaminant in the area you came from. You need to get dressed and leave now, we are about to go off shift."

"What? Nobody coming in to take over? I'm not sure I can stand," I wasn't being weak-willed. I didn't think I could support my own weight.

"No, they haven't shown up for the last three days."

"So, what if someone else needs your services?" I asked. They both shrugged and the younger one replied,

"That's up to the Authority." With one of them on either side of me, they tried to pull me up to a sitting position. My skin was raw, and I let out a yell of pain. I'd forgotten what this felt like.

"I can manage," I shouted and pulled my arms away from the two men. They had inflicted enough pain on me for a lifetime. I slowly dressed in the regulation patient uniform we used on the base. It covered everything, but the material was thin enough to make even the most body-confident person want to walk around with their hands in front of certain body parts.

The discharge process began. I was handed a tablet which displayed a list of all the items that had been credited to my account. My heart sank. They'd decontaminated my apartment and every fabric capable of harbouring a contaminant would be destroyed. The list alerted me to the fact that whatever food I'd had in my apartment had been removed. My clothes had gone. My bedding had gone. I was now expected to wander up to the supplies outlets and pick up the replacements. I was exhausted, the outlets weren't on the same levels of the station and I didn't know how I was expected to carry it all myself. My thoughts were interrupted by the older man's voice,

"You need to take two of these tablets in the morning and two before you go to sleep until they're finished."

Not that I cared at this point, but I asked anyway, "Will my hair fall out again?"

"No."

I raised an eyebrow. I guessed it was an improvement.

"Apply this ointment to the cuts once a day." I didn't make eye contact as I took the large tube of ointment from the younger man. I was aware of how many cuts I had. I hadn't looked too closely. I didn't need to, I could feel them all too well. Nodding and clasping my two new possessions, I walked towards the exit that only the cleansed were allowed to pass through. If the bright exit sign was there to make me feel uplifted, it failed.

I made both trips to food and to clothing which would also provide towels and bedding two hatches away. I'd need both in the morning. There was no point leaving one until later. I had the start of a headache. My knee was screaming. I wrapped the large towel around my waist over the embarrassing clothing. There was nowhere to change or I would have done. I had a bag of basic food in one hand and a bag of clothes and bedding in the other hand. I stooped. The decontamination process hadn't just ripped at my skin it had obliterated my energy. I looked at the corridor leading to the lift which I swear was moving further away. I wasn't sure I was going to make it. An expletive reached my ears from behind me. It took a couple of seconds for me to register it as a voice requiring attention. It was the kid. What was his name?

"Let me take that," he said and reached for the larger bag.

"I can manage," I barely got the words out. The bag dropped to the floor proving me wrong.

Laiten, that was his name. I felt him put an arm around my waist. I hissed as he aggravated a sore patch.

"Sorry," he said as he hefted the bag with his right arm and half carried me to the lift with his left.

I don't know how we made it.

"You were supposed to wait in decon for one of us to pick you up," he said as we reached my door.

"They closed up and kicked me out," I said as I staggered through my still open front door to see my apartment ransacked. The last thing I truly cared about on this hell-hole of a space station, Banyon, was in pieces in the middle of the floor.

5
In Bits

"Can you fix him?" Laiten asked as I stood over the remnants of my fake pet. I didn't care he wasn't a living, breathing dog. He was mine. He'd been in the family for years and he'd treated me better than some humans had. I stood for a few seconds and took some deep breaths. I was determined not to take my anger out on the kid who was doing his utmost to prove me wrong about my assumptions of most humans.

"How can you tell what he was? He's in bits," I lamented.

Laiten moved away to right some furniture as I meticulously retrieved Banyon bits from across the living room floor.

"I've heard about him. Plus," Laiten pointed, "fake fur. Must mean fake animal."

A thunk resonated as my large armchair regained its rightful position in the world. I carefully laid what looked like all of Banyon's parts on my dinner table. He was missing one eye.

"This wasn't just a decontamination, was it?" Laiten asked.

"No, I should say not," I replied, "Either this was malicious or someone was looking for something."

"What do you have that someone would want?" he asked.

"Nothing. There are a few pictures, personal stuff. Banyon. He's not worth anything. They made millions of them and they're still in circulation. He's just been with me for years." I attempted to pull another chair to the upright position but my arms were killing me and I dropped it.

"I've got this, sit down, you should be resting."

"You forgot to add 'old man' at the end."

Laiten laughed. "You're not old," he muttered.

"I feel it," I replied.

"Well, you're not. Do you have enough parts to put Banyon back together?"

"I think so. It'll take a while and he needed a service anyway," I said as Laiten finished relocating my furniture. From the other side of the room he called,

"Er Track, I have no idea what to do about this," he indicated the desk I jokingly called my 'workshop'. I felt slightly embarrassed. My workshop and I had done some good over the years. That did not detract from the fact it was an utter mess and always had been.

"Leave it," I said, "it was like that before whoever did this came in."

"Coffee?" he asked.

"Rum. Mix. There's a bottle in the fridge door. Help yourself to whatever you can find."

Laiten brought two large glasses over.

"Bottle's almost finished," he announced.

"S'OK, I can make some more. Thanks," I said taking the glass. "And thank you for doing all this. You didn't have to."

He shook his head, "No half-decent person would leave you in that state. I'll throw the covers on the bed in a minute and you can get some rest."

"I can do that," I said. We both knew I was lying.

Laiten took a large swig from his drink and I have to say I was impressed. He didn't choke. "This stuff is amazing. Where did you find it?" he asked.

It took me a while to answer. Even Jarner had winced when he drank some years ago. And he could down alcohol as well as I could. I shrugged. "It's just a mid-range rum with a concoction of things including something called 'caramel'."

"Is the recipe on the system?" he asked.

"Yes, I made it public last year," I paused. Was this my future? "I am not going to spend the next three months of my life swapping recipes with people." I tried to move out of my chair but failed. I reached for the pills I'd been given and threw two into my mouth. I followed them with a large swig of rum mix.

"Is that advisable?" Laiten asked.

I shrugged again. I hadn't thought to ask.

"I'm going to fix your bed, then I need to get back. Lena will be looking in the cells for me again."

"Girlfriend?" I asked.

"Wife," he replied. He read me like a book, laughed and said, "I'm not as young as I look. I'm thirty-seven and we've been married for six years," he smiled at my bemused expression. He continued, "Yeah, I know I look about twenty-three. I'm not. Chemical burns. They rebuilt my face, and this is what I ended up with. Don't spread that around. It's…"

I don't know how he intended to end that sentence. I finished with an assumption of my own, "Friends in high places? Must have cost a small fortune."

"Something like that."

So, my helper for the evening turned out to be a mere seven years younger than me. I had completely called that wrong and realised he'd not done a single thing to lead me to the conclusion he was younger, other than to look that way. I was reading the instructions on the tube of ointment when Laiten returned from making my bed.

"Do you need a hand with that?" he asked.

I shook my head.

"Should I at least check your back? You can't reach that on your own."

I was about to bite off a gruff "I can manage on my own" or something equally ungrateful. I stopped myself. He deserved to at least lay hands on such a great, desirable man as me. I was joking. Deflecting. Whatever I was thinking I removed my shirt, with help and noted the sharp intake of breath. Not because Laiten was in awe of my physique but because I could feel my back was ripped to shreds. He took the tube of ointment and gingerly rubbed some in.

"It's OK," I said, "I can feel it, but I've still got painkillers in my system. Just, go ahead."

"At least this is the new stuff. You'll heal faster."

"But not before the painkillers wear off," I sighed.

"Did they give you any more?" he asked.

"No, only the follow-up decontamination drugs. I should have some in the bedroom for my knee."

"You're going to need them later."

"No kidding," I muttered, noting they were already wearing off. I shivered. It wasn't cold in my apartment. The ointment wasn't particularly chilling. The only conclusions I could come to for this feeling were fatigue and shock.

"Do you need any help with anything else?" Laiten asked.

"No. You've done more than enough. Thank you," I replied.

"I'll come by and check on you in the morning. We can go to the desk and make this report together," he indicated my now tidy apartment and the Banyon bits on the table. "They'll need you as well as me. You know what it's like."

I tried to persuade him it wasn't necessary. I failed. He closed the door behind him and I felt cold, alone and sorry for myself. Jarner would have kicked my arse again. Gently, given the circumstances, but he'd have done it. Against my better judgement, I downed the rest of the rum and retrieved the shirt I'd discarded earlier. I staggered into my bedroom via a wall and two chairs whose presence stopped me from collapsing to the floor.

My back glowed as did the rest of me as I squeezed some more ointment onto my battered skin. For the first time, I caught a glimpse of my face in the bedroom mirror and twisted around to see who was behind me. No-one. I barely recognised myself. My face was red and puffy. I thought I was having difficulty opening my eyes because they were tired. But no, my eyelids were severely swollen. "Fuck sake.

Laiten, you poor bastard. Sorry you had to be a witness to this monstrosity," I said out loud. Not that I was in the market, but I was not going to be pulling any handsome men anytime soon. I'd give a kid nightmares with just one look.

I had to look away. The swelling in my face would go down. If I could get cream on my cuts, they would heal quicker. To coin a phrase, it should all look better in the morning.

I systematically coated myself with gunk whilst sitting on the side of my bed. It soaked in quickly, I fell asleep twice before I'd finished. Finally, I put the tube on the bedside table and retrieved my painkillers from my drawer. The decon centre painkillers wouldn't fully wear off for another few hours. Laiten had thoughtfully provided me with a glass of water. I hated water, but true to form could not be bothered to change it to something more palatable. I put the water and the drugs within late-night groping distance and made a cacophony of sounds as I manipulated myself into bed.

***

It was late. It was dark, and I had no business being awake. I checked the time and closed my eyes briefly when I saw it was the early hours of the morning. I listened for any indication of what had woken me. There was nothing. In the hope the painkillers would aid more sleep I took a dose and grimaced as I tasted the metallic water I washed them down with.

The glass made a sound as I returned it to the table. I was convinced I heard something else at exactly that moment. I closed my eyes and listened. There was someone in the kitchen. The rest of my apartment was an open plan room and I could hear the chink of kitchen utensils from the other end.

I threw back the bedclothes and retrieved my backup weapon from my bedside table as silently as I could. I managed to stifle the yell that accompanied further movement from my battered body. It all hurt. I slipped my feet into my shoes. My soles were sore.

The living area was in darkness. I sensed rather than saw someone at the far end. My plan had been to close the gap between the intruder and my front door, trapping him, if it was a him. It was too dark to tell. My knee took it upon itself to twinge at exactly that moment. My intake of breath was too loud. I heard movement from the other end of my apartment. My eyes took too long to adjust to the darkness. I was at a disadvantage. I sensed someone move towards the door.

"Stop, I'm armed," I warned. Ducking, I avoided the pulse of light from the intruder's weapon. So much for manners. I shouldn't have bothered with the warning. My attempt to hit them went wide as they made it to the door. I fired again with no faith I'd hit my target. I limped awkwardly to the door ignoring the pain in my knee. As I looked in the corridor, I could make out a dark figure rounding the corner to the service lifts. I gave chase more for pride than with any hope of catching up.

The lights overhead flickered, and I lumbered on a few more feet. I didn't get far before I heard a voice behind me.

"I heard shots. What the hell is going on?" Mr Annoying Neighbour again. I will never understand why people hear shots in the night and think it's an awesome idea to poke their heads outside into what might be the line of fire. In my heightened fight mode, I swung around and pointed my weapon at him before turning back towards my prey. My neighbour didn't even flinch. I gave up. I wasn't going to catch the dark figure. I limped back to placate my neighbour. Why I would, was beyond me. He might have been responsible for the destruction of Banyon. He was whinging about going through the completely pain-free, non-event of the new decontamination procedure. I hate whingers, which is rich coming from someone currently holding a glossy brown Filtium medal in whinging.

"I'm fine, thank you for asking," I said, dripping sarcasm. "Who did that," I asked, indicating a dark bruise on the front of his left shoulder. He pulled his robe closed and didn't answer. This action reminded me I was armed and half-naked in the corridor, still wearing the trousers they'd given me in decon that didn't leave anything to the imagination. Splendid.

6
Dismissed

Hammering inside my head. No. Not inside my head. What is that? It took a few seconds for me to realise the gunfire annihilating my husband's body and forcing him to perform a macabre dance was a dream. False memories of his battered body jerking to the ground subsided. I only imagined that was his fate. I had no proof. I was merely informed he had died.

I was awake. The hammering persisted. My bedroom lights were doing their utmost to bring me back to the land of the living. My system stalled for a while as I forgot mornings were for getting out of bed. I thought about it. Then I wondered what the point was. Hammering. It hadn't stopped. Memories of last night's antics drifted into my brain as I threw back the covers. I peeled my healing skin away from the bottom sheet with a suitably disgusted look on my face. I took three steps forwards until my knee threatened to give out on me. Hopping, I hoped the chip would kick in and enable me some movement and stability.

On the way out of my bedroom, I grabbed my robe. Whoever was at the door did not need to see me in the trousers that may as well not be there, certainly not first thing in the morning.

"I'm coming, hang on," I yelled. It wasn't my fault it sounded so gruff. I hadn't had coffee yet. I made it to the door via a few pieces of furniture I staggered into. "Laiten, morning," I said as I opened the door and impressed myself with my ability to remember his name. The least I could do is feign friendliness after his assistance the previous night. He held up a bag in each hand.

"Lena made us breakfast," he said.

"She didn't need to do that."

"She insisted," he said as I made way for him. He gave the Banyon bits on the table a forlorn look as he laid out the food at the opposite end.

"I'll make coffee," I growled. My voice still had not reached human levels.

"You should know there has been another noise complaint against you," Laiten said as he started breakfast without me.

"What now?" I began, before groaning as I realised.

"Neighbour reported hearing gunshots from this apartment last night. He only reported it half an hour ago which is why I was banging on your door." He paused to brush crumbs from his uniform as I placed a mug of coffee in front of him. He added whitener and sweetener from the tray I'd brought in. "Thought you were injured when you didn't answer straight away. Your neighbour neglected to include any details other than the noise disturbance."

"That's all he's interested in," I said through a mouthful of baked breakfast muffin.

"These are fantastic. Did Lena bake these herself?" I asked.

"I believe she opened the packaging and put them in the oven, yes," he replied. I smiled, acquiring raw ingredients was virtually impossible. Everything was pre-made or partially made.

"Tell her I truly appreciate the effort," I said.

"Tell her yourself," Laiten began, "she wants you around for dinner."

I began my usual "can't", "won't", "rubbish company right now" speech. Laiten listened with amusement for a few seconds before ignoring me and saying,

"There's no point arguing. Either we'll eat at our place, or she'll bring the whole shebang here. Best thing to do is turn up, eat, spend an hour or two and go home. You'll get a couple of weeks reprieve before she starts insisting again."

"Anything for a quiet life?" I asked. Laiten smiled.

"She's going through a rough patch, like everyone else. She can't have kids and wants them. Lena needs someone to look after and I'm pretty self-sufficient. She sees you as convalescing after the bout in decontamination."

"She's not wrong," I replied. I relented. I felt I owed him, "OK we'll set a day and time," I said.

"Tonight," Laiten announced.

"OK, we'll set tonight. I can survive one night on my own," I complained.

"Humour me."

We'd finished all the baked goods and the coffee and began clearing away. I saw Laiten out of the corner of my eye and suddenly thought I was looking at Jarner. They were similar in build but Laiten's face was completely different. I closed my eyes and shook the notion from my mind. Laiten's face wasn't his own, but that didn't make him my late husband. Besides, there was the whole married to a woman issue. Jarner was most definitely gay.

"We ought to get going. Beynard will require a report on the weapon's discharge from last night," Laiten said.

"I don't suppose he's bothered if I was shot or not?" I quipped.

"Probably not," Laiten said, honestly.

I wandered towards my bedroom and was surprised Laiten followed me. "Er, boundaries?" I looked at him with wide eyes. I'd never been a man to let it all hang out in the locker room with other men.

"Sorry, I should use my words more. Can I put more of that ointment on your back for you?"

"I could kill for a shower," I said.

"You can't," he replied.

"I know, I need to heal more," I passed him the ointment and peeled my robe away from my skin. It was Jarner's hands I felt on my back. I knew that was nonsense. If I didn't want to lose myself in a preposterous fantasy, I was going to have to stamp that notion out once and for all. Maybe I should thump him.

"Fuck's sake," I muttered out loud.

"What's wrong?" Laiten's hand stopped, and he passed the tube back to me.

"Nothing, I'm wallowing in self-pity and finding it pathetic."

If words could hang in the air, they would have said, "You said it, not me."

"I'll wait in the living room." Laiten began, "please find some other trousers to wear than those. You look like a hooker in the gay bar I busted last year."

"Bastard, I like that place."

"Drug dealing."

"Oh, fair enough," I called as I found my new clothes. Someone had taken pity on me and issued post-old-style decontamination clothing. Nothing was scratchy, and it was all coated on the inside to not stick to healing skin. I was honoured. I slapped ointment on the worst bits. It was likely to be the quickest recovery I'd experienced and possibly my last application. I was relieved. Picking bits of skin off my bed sheets wasn't my idea of a fun morning.

"Let's see what our leader has to say," I quipped as I left the bedroom.

My new skin felt tight as we made our way to the lift. As we descended, one of the few children on the station dropped her teddy bear on the floor of the lift. It had lost its fur. The metal of the toy clanged loudly on the metal of the lift floor. I spotted the legs the girl had been issued. They were not conducive to bending to the floor even if she was only a couple of feet away from it. I reached down and let out the biggest 'old man' groan I had issued to date. My skin felt like it might split. How I'd initiated a chase last night I'd never know. Laiten bent forward and retrieved the toy.

"Say thank you," the mother instructed. She too was staggering on artificial limbs. I counted myself lucky.

"Thank you," the girl replied, not making eye-contact with Laiten. The garish lights of the education floor hurt my eyes as the doors of the lift opened.

The Authority had done their best to accommodate and educate the youngsters on the station. They had essential food and clothes and were taught reading, writing and vocational skills. Hopefully, these would give them a chance to stand on their own prosthetic feet later in life. The Authority had a reputation to maintain. They expected their students to achieve.

Laiten waved to a tall blonde woman. She smiled and waved back. I could tell from looking at her she had been ravished by the contamination outbreak. She had a grey pallor and short stringy hair. Her face was thin, yet her lips were full and probably either coated in makeup or shot full of implant. I didn't need any introductions. The loving look on Laiten's face said it all. This was Lena. She called over to me,

"See you tonight," as the doors closed.

"So that's where she gets her supplies from?" I asked.

"They're given an allowance. Since the drought on the Mato Three farming colony, the Authority has been attempting to create backup food supplies using alternative raw ingredients. One of Lena's jobs on the side is to make the alternative palatable. I groaned, suspecting the worst.

"What did I eat this morning?" I asked as I fixed him with my best disapproving stare. He grinned.

"It's perfectly safe and highly nutritious. Insects probably. A section of Mato Three was devastated by a beetle infestation. Turns out, they're edible."

"So, what? You ate our grain, we'll eat you, you bastards?" I asked.

"Yep, pretty much. All because a kid got out into a swarm, and one flew into her mouth. They collected some in a panic, assuming they were poisonous. Nothing happened to the girl. The bugs were deemed harmless and even nutritious."

"And we don't know about this why?" I asked.

"They're bugs. Nothing wrong with them. Very good for you. But they're still bugs. People would riot!"

"Doubt they have the energy," I said as the doors opened on the blue and grey of the Authority Four HQ.

Half a dozen people in the public area, wasted their time waiting to be seen. I recognised them. Their complaints had been taken, reviewed and closed. It was the only reason people repeated a trip to the desk; they didn't agree with the outcome.

We skirted the area and headed straight through the Authority entrance. My knee twinged. I fell a step behind Laiten as the room fell silent. Wicklow raised a hand in greeting. The silence merely prevented me hearing any details I was no longer allowed to.

Laiten knocked on Beynard's door and waited to be let in. Beynard waved at us through the glass.

"Sit," he barked as we entered. I couldn't help myself, I let out a surreptitious "woof" as I parked my arse on the seat. Laiten sniggered. I looked up with as straight a face as I could muster and saw Beynard glaring at me.

"Noise disturbance, shots fired in your apartment, last night. Explain," he snapped.

"Just that," I began. "There was an intruder, we exchanged fire. He or she escaped."

"And you didn't think to report it?" he asked.

I contemplated a few responses before settling on one which would cause the least amount of offence. "I was recovering from the decontamination process and I was exhausted. I wasn't thinking straight." The *I'm getting better now, thank you for asking,* was more effective at rattling Beynard's cage muttered under my breath. It received another glare.

"Description?"

"None. Well, hooded, dark clothes, fast. Probably a similar height and build to me," I replied.

"Mundanely average," Beynard uttered the words as he

entered them into the system. Someone had crawled out of the wrong side of the bed.

"What about the woman who died at my apartment?" I asked.

"All I can tell you is her name was Olivian and Medical suspect she died from a complication from the prosthesis," Beynard answered.

I screwed my face up but refrained from slamming my hand on Beynard's desk. "People don't die from a complication from an artificial limb. That's ridiculous," I exclaimed.

"They can do if they have an infection that goes untreated."

"I don't buy it," I said. "Why did she seek my help earlier in the day if she was sick with something? No-one would expect me to be able to help in that situation. She sought me out specifically. It cannot be as simple as that."

"The medical report says it can," Beynard countered.

"What? Already? Can I see it?"

"No. You are relieved of duty. It is none of your concern. Stay out of it. That particular investigation is closed."

"But…" I began.

Beynard cut me off. "We're done here. Go and take a course at the COC."

"Hang-on," I interrupted, "the break-in to my apartment while I was in decon?"

Beynard waved a hand at me but wouldn't maintain eye-contact, "That was the decontamination process of your apartment, not a break-in."

I shook my head, "No, it wasn't. My place was ransacked and Banyon is in bits. One of his eyes is missing."

"So, they were careless."

"No, what about the intruder? There's a witness for that one," I complained.

"I'll assign someone to look into it," Beynard stared directly at me.

I resisted the urge to tell him he was all heart.

"You may leave."

Laiten and I both stood. I hobbled towards the door.

"Laiten, stay."

I left the room hiding another bark in a cough.

The outer room was silent again as I walked through towards the exit. Wicklow called out, "Catch up with you soon."

I waved in her direction. As the door closed behind me, I could hear the muffled background noise resume.

***

I made my way back to my apartment to rebuild Banyon. I closed the apartment door behind me and listened for any unusual sounds. Hearing nothing, I retrieved my only spare Banyon eye from the drawer of my workshop. As I turned to count the Banyon bits on the table, Banyon's remaining, non-interactive eye flashed at me. It looked like it would explode.

7

We Can Rebuild You

I stood paralysed as I assessed the flashing red light in Banyon's disconnected eyeball. They just didn't do that. Banyon's eyes didn't even swivel, let alone flash. It occurred to me that it might be some form of explosive. It was smaller than any advanced technology we'd come across recently. That didn't mean that a company hadn't created something like it. No. I wasn't buying it. I wasn't sure if that was a wise move. It reminded me of something else. For my next questionable action, I picked the damn thing up and put it to my eye to see if there was anything inside. If it was an explosive and went off at that moment I'd probably lose my head before I got the chance to lose my mind during eighty-nine days of enforced leave.

Guess what? It didn't explode. I had nowhere safe to keep it. There were no shielded containers in my apartment. Having all but convinced myself it wouldn't obliterate the entire station, as I sat down to rebuild my pet dog, my gaze was constantly drawn to the flashing eyeball on the table in front of me. It didn't change. It kept up its uniform pattern of two flashes per second.

"Dammit," I muttered, which was quite restrained for me. Banyon's voice module was broken. Whereas I had a pretty good idea where I could find a replacement for my pet dog, a spare did not live in my workshop. I had to make do with a different animal. The shame!

"Well, you've got four legs, a tail, a head, a voice of sorts and one eye. It's the best I can do for now," I said to Banyon who made what I tried to convince myself was a barking noise. "That eye-socket is grizzly," I grinned. I've always liked the macabre. "Hang on, though," I muttered. As I walked over to my workshop Banyon followed. I rummaged around spilling various parts of who knew what across the long desk. "Aha, gotcha, I wonder if I can get this to fit. Here boy," I said unnecessarily as he followed me back to the dining room table. I'd have used the actual workshop desk if it hadn't been covered in accumulated random tech.

I sat down and grabbed Banyon and put him on the table in front of me. The power source in the spare eye was fine. It took a bit of fiddling to insert it into the sockets with my big, clumsy fingers. Eventually, I won.

I patted Banyon on the head and he 'barked'. I laughed out loud. "You'll have to do," I said as Banyon utilised his new voice and his new eye glowed a menacing pure red at me. "Banyon the Hell Dog. I'm taking you with me tonight, it'll give me something to talk about."

Banyon 'barked' again.

"That voice has got to go, so undignified," I commiserated with my pet. "Right, listen, I'm going to have to power you down while I go out." Banyon attempted to whine with his new voice module. It was more of a hiss and was just plain wrong. "I know you hate it, but I don't want whoever broke in to have another go at you. It's for your own good."

I had nothing totally secure, but I could put him out of sight. I switched him off. I hadn't done that for a reason other than maintenance for years. I couldn't look at his lifeless body. I couldn't acknowledge Banyon was temporarily 'gone'. *He was a sodding robot.* Since Jarner died, Hegland was undercover, and I'd all but lost my job, who did I have? Who did I interact with the most? A robot dog and a barman whose arm kept falling off. I shuddered. An overwhelming sense of loneliness penetrated my thoughts. I felt a spiral of despair looming in the future. No. I was not alone. The station housed plenty of other people. We outnumbered the automatons.

I had errands to run, and I decided to get a drink at the bar when I'd finished them. The bar with the robot barman - there really was no hope.

I looked over at the flashing eyeball. No change. No sparks, no explosions. As I purposely refused to look at Banyon, I blindly grabbed him, took him into the bedroom and placed him in the lockable cupboard. I locked him in and leant my head against the door thinking a silent apology to my fake dog. *Not a real dog. Fake dog. He had no feelings on the matter. Get a grip.*

I pocketed my newly acquired flashing eyeball. I checked the flashing light was not visible through the fabric of my trousers. I wasn't after that kind of attention. As I reached my front door I had a second thought and headed back to the cupboard in the bedroom. After dragging out my wheeled case and heading to the door, I hoped the wheels would behave once they had weight on them. The bugger kept tipping from side to side.

With my front door open, I almost fell headlong over a vacuum-packed pile of spare bedding and towels. Must be a new service. I'd never had deliveries after the last decontamination events. Grateful to throw the old case aside, I dragged the bedding inside and left. Grunting, I managed to get my arm through the doorway to retrieve my backpack before the door attempted an amputation. Never trust the door sensors.

As I walked towards the lifts, I heard a noise behind me. Weariness in my knee slowed my movements, but I stopped and turned. No-one there. The lights flickered. "And you can piss off," I muttered at the lights. Clearly, I had no telekinetic powers or psychic ability - they flickered again out of spite.

My weapon hadn't left my side all day, and I was reassured by its presence. Had it been taken away I'd probably have gone black-market and armed myself that way. *There's nobody there,* I thought as I walked towards the lifts. A few hours had done wonders for my skin. The tightening effect of the ointment had worn off and if there was a little girl in the lift to drop a toy on the floor, I probably would have been able to help.

I reached my desired floor and headed towards the clothes outlet. Another lift opened behind me. I looked over my shoulder. No-one. They could have got out and gone around the corner before I looked, I told myself.

The clothes outlet was never busy. Fabrics were made to last. No-one had anywhere to go other than work and a few leisure establishments. I needed my quota of underwear, maybe something to exercise in and some daywear. I'd pick up a new uniform if I'd been cleared to receive one.

I caught a moving shape out of the corner of my eye. I turned and once again, saw nothing. I was not aware of any side effects from decontamination or the medication I'd been given that would lead to hallucinations. Either I'd picked up a tail, or I was paranoid.

A sound on the other side of me caused me to reach for my weapon.

"Can I help you, Track?"

"For fuck's sake," I muttered under my breath. Service robot, it was only a service robot.

I don't know why we kept up the pretence of being scanned for ID and bringing up our allowances on the screen. The robots were a part of the same system and had instant access to our lists of allowable consumables. I guess it was to fool us into believing we had some sort of control over our lives.

We danced the dance and stared at each other while my clothes were retrieved from behind the walls. They were piled neatly onto the counter. What? Were you expecting racks of clothes I could choose from? Maybe a different shade of this or a different cut of that? You'll be thinking of bigger and better places. Those to the left and right of Si-Cross Four. They did their best. The walls displayed smiley people wearing various apparel. I assumed they took the pictures elsewhere. No-one on Si-Cross Four looked that healthy. I checked through my pile of designated clothing and noted an obvious absence.

"What, no uniform?" I asked the robot.

"You are not currently eligible for an Authority Four uniform. You may, however, have an extra pair of underpants. They are gold in colour." He held them up. The robots were not known for their humour. But this guy seriously had to be kidding.

"Since when am I an exotic dancer?" I asked.

"You do not like your bonus underpants?" he asked.

"Those are not pants. I've seen more fabric on a wristband!"

"I can't even give them away," he complained in a staccato voice.

Something behind me caught the robot's eye, and he paused. I turned and saw nothing.

"What? What did you see?" I felt like grabbing his shoulders and shaking him but refrained.

"Nothing. Will there be anything else?" he asked.

"Am I entitled to anything else?"

"No."

I could have smacked him. I gave him a stare and stuffed my clothes into my backpack.

"Remember Nartern Eleven."

My head shot up as he finished the words. "What did you say?"

"I'm sorry?" he replied.

"Repeat the last thing you said before 'I'm sorry,'" I instructed.

"The last thing I said to you was 'no'"

"Nothing else?" I asked.

"Nothing else."

I could hear the blood rushing in my ears. Nartern Eleven did not exist. It was a nickname Jarner and I had given to a place we'd secretly visited once. No-one else knew about our visit but us. I had never divulged that name to anyone. It was so insignificant, I was sure Jarner wouldn't either. And Jarner was dead.

Stomping wasn't a good action for my knee, but I couldn't help it. I needed to be away from the robot. I went back to the lifts convinced someone was following me. I caught nothing more than a shadow whenever I turned to confront whoever was tailing me.

When in the solitary confinement of the lift, I hit the button for the food level. *Our* food level, not the VIP one. Ours was a depressing, run-down area of too many people, not enough food and despite the sterile interior, gave me a yearning for a shower. As soon as the door opened my nostrils were filled with sumptuous smells which, although fake, made us feel hope that what we were about to receive would have a corresponding flavour. Our daily food was nothing like Lena's bug muffins.

I joined the shortest queue. Surrounding walls showed pictures of various food options on flickering screens. A few faulty screens skewed their images and one looked like a family was enjoying a bloodbath rather than a meal. The image distracted me from the banality of waiting in line. It was a busy time of day for food. Dejected workers often picked up their family's food allowance at this time so they had their evening meals and breakfast already to hand. During times of preparation for visiting dignitaries, our food was rationed to a once a day supply while manufacturing worked on building up stock for VIPs. This was one such time. We stood. We waited. My knee made me want to swear. I swore in frustration under my breath. It did not make me feel any better.

I scanned the queues for anything suspicious. It was all normal. Gradually, the people in front of me retrieved their orders with a mixture of relief and exhaustion and I made it to the glistening counter. I was scanned and awaited my food list. Some of it had the option to change one or two flavours Usually what was on offer was good enough. I read my list as it appeared on the horizontal silver counter screen in front of me. Glancing left and right I was relieved I couldn't see anyone else's list, so they couldn't read mine. It contained two words, "Nartern Eleven."

"What is this?" I looked up from the countertop and growled at the service robot.

"These are your usual choices. Please look again," he insisted.

I looked down. Evening meal, breakfast, lunch, as I wasn't working at the moment and wouldn't be fed at Authority Four. No mention of Nartern Eleven. I could hear pounding in my ears again and my heart appeared to be beating in different places inside my chest.

"Please make any alterations to your choices."

I pressed a few buttons and used my surplus to acquire a dessert for that evening, aware that if it wasn't needed, it'd keep until later.

I felt eyes on me from all directions. But no-one was paying me any attention. I bagged up my goods and left the noise of the food queues. Weaving my way through the occupied grey tables and chairs, I glanced at the diners assessing them for the criminal intent I had no ability to sense. A child sang loudly in the corner of the room to the amusement of the adults at the neighbouring tables. I would have given anything to get away from robots and screens, but I needed a drink.

I breathed a sigh of relief as I entered Ethan's Ol' Bar. It always had the feel of a sanctuary of sorts. Even with the inevitable occasional bar brawl. Apart from losing touch with a limb now and then, Ethan never faltered. He was a constant I found myself relying on. I had no idea how unhealthy that was. "Dammit," I said, "Ethan I forgot to look for the attachment pin. I'll look later and bring it around. I'm sure I have one."

Ethan's head jolted towards me as he stood behind the bar.

"Hello, Track. Do you remember Nartern Eleven?"

8
Too Many People

I admit, with yet another mention of the mythical Nartern Eleven, I felt dizzy. I had been informed Jarner was dead. No matter how much I wanted that to be a blatant lie, I'd been trying to come to terms with it for what felt like a lifetime.

Nartern Eleven could only mean one of two things. Either my dead husband was alive and trying to send me a message. Or someone had overheard our pillow-talk and was trying to… what? If unnerving me was the goal, guess what, you bastards, you damn well succeeded.

I heard a noise in front of me. It was the comical sound of a robotic voice attempting to clear its throat as Ethan attracted my attention. I dismissed his initial question and put one of my own,

"Ethan, why did you ask me about Nartern Eleven?"

"Sorry, Track, I have no recollection of asking you about Nartern Eleven. I am not aware of its existence. Where or what is it?"

"It doesn't matter. I'd love a rum, please."

As Ethan prepared my drink, I looked around. I was either paranoid or diligently security conscious. The jury was still out. And I was no closer to determining the reason for the Nartern Eleven messages no-one other than me seemed to hear.

I came to from my mental list of possible theories as my drink sloshed over my hand. It was another reminder I had some mechanics to take care of. "Thanks, Ethan. I promise I will fix your arm." I scanned for payment. A face I did not recognise appeared beside me.

"Beer," he instructed.

I know I have a knack for getting into trouble. I know I never learn. I turned to face the newcomer. "Rough day?" I asked, politely.

He snorted and turned to face Ethan,

"Come on robot. Move," he said in a louder voice. He was probably a stereotypical lout of self-importance, who wrongly assumed the worlds were there to serve him. I held my tongue. To many people, the service robots were just there to serve. They weren't to be engaged with or shown any consideration. It was a cold-hearted arsehole who didn't once or twice find themselves interacting with them as if they were human. Some more recent models were given faces and hands to resemble ours. Their skin colour was wrong, but these days only the human VIPs managed a healthy glow.

Si-Cross Four's human population had a grey hue to their skin. The bots with humanoid faces, purple. The lights in the bar made some of the patchwork repairs to Ethan's face glow. He had been an upgrade. And frankly, a poor one. The original head shape was wrong for the face someone had manhandled onto it. Of course, in that respect, I only had myself to blame!

"You fucking cretin, in the glass, not on me." The obnoxious customer hissed.

"That's no way to speak to an ailing service bot in desperate need of maintenance," I countered.

"And, who the fuck are you?" he asked.

What was I? Don't say friend. Whatever you do, do not say friend. "Just an off-duty Authority Four detective in need of a quiet drink."

The arsehole snorted again, grudgingly scanned for his drink and left for a booth. I mentally patted myself on my healing back for avoiding more of a confrontation.

"Thank you for defending me, Track."

"No problem," I said and stopped with my glass halfway to my lips. I was about to say something, but Ethan had slipped into standby mode and I decided to let him get on with his duties. Ethan's model had been programmed with language skills and the ability to give out the odd free drink to someone who showed them consideration. It amounted to a loyalty scheme but gave them a friendlier personality. They could react and stop a bar brawl to keep the peace and avoid harm to humans but were supposed to ignore insulting behaviour towards themselves. I clearly had spent too much time with Ethan over the years and tried to push his pseudo-friendship out of my mind.

I had to decide who to trust. I knocked back my drink and ran through some names in my head. It was a short list. I stopped tapping the glass on the bar, rapped my hands on the surface and said, "I'll be back later–this time with a new pin, I promise."

"Goodbye Track," Ethan replied. A small corner of synthetic skin was peeling away from his face. That was going to cause an argument if it dropped into someone's drink. I grinned and left the bar hoping a certain someone encountered face with their next beer.

***

I rounded the corner towards the public lifts and was met with a crowd. There were a lot of grim looking people waiting. Part of me thought about staying with them for the safety in numbers effect. The anti-social bastard in me turned around, just as someone in the middle did a double take at me. Nope, not in the mood. I decided to test if my access to the service lifts was still valid.

Inside, as I watched the floor numbers go by on the screen, I blinked. The numbers changed to letters. N.A.R.T I turned away for a few seconds. When I braved the screen again E.L.E.V.E.N. I stared. Fatigue enveloped me like a length of heavy chains. Moving would be a struggle. What did it mean? Either I was being particularly dense or... well, I couldn't reach another conclusion. But I refused to build up my hopes of ever seeing my husband again.

I had my hand on my gun as the door opened. Half-expecting the latest message to precede a gun battle, I was quite disappointed to walk out of the lift into a deserted hallway. I stood and listened for a few seconds but could hear nothing other than the usual hum and drone of the station's mechanics.

I walked towards my neighbours' door and was about to knock and check on the old man until I remembered he'd been dead for months. Mentally, I was not at my best. Physically, I felt obsolete. Instead of knocking, I recoiled, glad I had not alerted my new neighbours to my presence. Like a naughty child, I moved quickly towards my door.

Inside, I squashed my backpack between me and my closed door until my back itched and I remembered the bag contained food as well as clothes. The delayed reaction from the latest message kicked in, and I pressed a hand against my chest. I took a deep breath. I looked around for Banyon and remembered I'd locked him in the cupboard. I felt wrong. But if anyone had asked me, I wouldn't have been able to phrase it any better.

My best course of action was to accomplish something, no matter how small. I removed my backpack and carefully laid it on the table. My apartment looked untouched. I retrieved Banyon and booted him up. His 'bark' took me by surprise. "Soon, I promise I'll get you a new voice as soon as I can," I told him. His tail appeared to wag slower since I restarted him.

Having stowed my food and clothes and made sure the dessert was in one piece, I started the shower. I stopped the shower and swore. I still had at least another night of healing to do before I could soak my skin. I freshened up as best I could and changed my shirt. My back didn't look too bad in the mirror.

Next, I tried to get hold of Wicklow. No answer. I thought about leaving a message, but she had enough to worry about without me adding to it. Rummaging around on my desk, I found not one, but two pins that should fit Ethan's arm assembly.

Armed with my weapon, attachment pins and dessert, I called out, "Come on boy," and Banyon joined me at the door. Comms informed me where I was going for dinner and as luck would have it, we arrived on time and with no incident.

Laiten opened the door to a far cheerier apartment than the one I'd just left. "Hey, you brought Banyon. Glad you could fix him."

Lena approached as we were shown into the living area. "Aw, he's very cute. Love the red eye. I take it that's not the original?" she asked.

Banyon used his new voice in reply. Both Laiten and Lena stared wide-eyed at Banyon and then at me before Lena asked, "Why does your dog sound like a cat?"

"I'm calling it an alternative bark. I know, the shame. Poor Banyon. I know where I can get him a new voice module." I handed Lena the dessert box, "I wasn't sure what to bring, but this looked interesting," my tone was hopeful.

"I love these," she exclaimed, "I'll put it in the heater after dinner. They don't take long. After a few minutes, we'll see what shape it is. I haven't had one in ages. Thank you."

"You're welcome. I see Banyon is drawn to your fire graphic," I said as my robot dog made himself comfortable in front of Laiten and Lena's flickering log fire effect.

"I chose it," Lena said, "Laiten wanted the rampaging big cat design. It tears apart a deer for your amusement."

I nodded. I'd seen it. We gathered around Banyon on comfortable seats.

The silence was relaxed until Lena stood, "A few more minutes until dinner," she returned to the kitchen.

"She insisted on cooking this one herself. We do usually share the cooking," Laiten said.

I reached into my pocket. "What do you make of this?" I passed the item over. I figured it was more useful confiding in him than Ethan. Despite knowing nothing about him,

Laiten was all I had at that moment.

"Banyon's eye?"

"Yes. I thought it might explode at first, but I'm pretty sure it's something else."

Laiten jiggled with the attachment behind the eyeball while I hoped my assumption was correct. The 'optic nerve' detached. I winced but just heard, "Aha, thought so. Messaging device or a storage device. I've got nothing here I can read this with," Laiten said passing the eyeball back.

The eyeball was tangible. I decided against telling him about my Nartern Eleven messages.

"That's OK, thanks. I may know someone," I said.

We ate a delicious meal, the ingredients of which I was too much of a coward to ask about. Lena heated the dessert and squealed when she brought it to us.

"Look, it's a blue tree. I haven't seen one of those in ages."

Sure enough, the dessert had expanded into an edible model of a blue tree. I couldn't begin to tell you how it held its shape or why the result was kept a secret on the packaging. It tasted nice enough. I think the manufacturers were going for the look rather than the flavour.

We chatted for a while about trivial matters. It was pleasant to leave dead bodies and break-ins behind. But, I wasn't really in the mood for small talk. I wanted to hobble into action. I thanked them both far too many times for lack of something to say.

With Banyon at my side, I stopped as I was leaving and asked, "Have they done anything about the dead woman, Olivian, at my apartment? Or my break-in?"

"Not now," Laiten said looking over his shoulder to check Lena was out of ear-shot. "I'll come around and talk to you tomorrow. I don't like Lena getting caught up in Authority business. Beynard did say I was to encourage you to go to the COC."

I groaned aloud and heard the door close as I walked away. Without even thinking where I was going, and with a cursory glance down to my companion, I found myself entering the bar again.

The shock of the late evening crowd woke me from my thoughts. I picked Banyon up and carried him to the bar. He was allowed in, but I didn't trust the oafs with big feet around him. "What's going on?" I asked, shouldering my way to the front where I could hear the raised voices of an argument. Ethan swung his body from side to side and I noticed the lack of arm.

"Everybody shut up and let me deal with this." I opened the door to the bar, "Get out," I grabbed the so-called adult responsible for swinging Ethan around and threw him out of the robot's space one-handed.

"How old are you?" I asked as I closed the door. I gave the crowd a suitably impatient, disapproving look and set Banyon on the floor.

It took a couple of minutes to reattach Ethan's arm with the correct pin. I stood back and watched with satisfaction as he sped his way through the backlog of drinks orders. As the last drink was served, I turned to look at Ethan and sighed, watching patrons drift to the corners of the bar.

"Thank you, Track. Please allow me to pour you a drink on the house." He didn't wait for confirmation. I had already decided I wasn't staying. The rowdy atmosphere wasn't what I sought that night. I downed my drink and thanked the barman.

With Banyon in my arms, I made my way through the maze of workers in various stages of inebriation. In the back of my mind, I'd established a plan for Banyon's flashing eye that I wanted to put into action.

***

Despite keeping my senses alert for my elusive tail from earlier, I detected nothing. The door at the end of the corridor was locked. I knocked. I heard shuffling and scrambling but the door remained closed.

The thing about techs is that they are always tinkering with something at random hours. I knew they were in there and thumped the door again, "Come on, open up, it's Track. I brought Banyon," I said as an incentive. I heard a thunk, and the door opened. "Call yourself techs? You still haven't fixed the camera at your door!" I complained to Shifton, the bald woman of indeterminate age who was on her own that night. I didn't make the mistake of complimenting her on her cautiousness in opening the door. She was a lethal entity, highly competent in many forms of combat. A nuke might stop her, but that was about it.

I put Banyon on the floor and he immediately joined the capybara robot at the other end of the room and 'barked.'

"What have you done to Banyon?" Shifton asked, disgust evident in her voice.

"Long story, but yes, I'll take a module if you have one."

Shifton's spares desk was similar to mine. She found a replacement and handed it to me. I thanked her, and she stared at me expectantly.

"I need you to look at this," I said, handing her the flashing eyeball.

"Awesome, dog-cam. These went out ages ago." She inserted the gadget into one of the slots her desk was equipped with.

"Hmmm, it's not dangerous. But, whatever is on here is corrupt or bad quality. It's going to take some time to clean up. Due to its age, it won't be great when I've finished with it."

"Whatever you can do, Shif, I appreciate it."

"I can tell you the time and date and it looks like a visual recording." She pointed to the screen.

"Watch your back with this," I warned, "that is the time and date my apartment was ransacked while I was being decontaminated."

In true Shifton style, she ignored my warning and went straight for the potential, "So, the intruder might be on this. Something else I can tell you—these devices can be activated remotely. Don't know if that helps."

"Can't think who would want to do that."

"If you activate it, you can set it for motion detection too."

"Maybe they know," I began.

"Huh?"

"Banyon's red eye," I said.

Shifton chuckled, "I noticed. Nice touch."

"It was either that or an empty socket. Banyon was dismantled and one of his eyes taken. Maybe whoever took it assumed they'd got this one. They wouldn't have known, it didn't start flashing until the day after I came home from decon. After I was broken into."

"You sure about that?" she asked, "decon can mess you up."

"Positive. Let me know as soon as you have anything. But, Shif, be careful. I've been followed all day. I raised my eyebrows at her piqued interest and left her to it, calling Banyon as I went.

***

I yawned as I went back to my apartment. The corridors were busy with plenty of people making their own way home. I was reassured by their presence until I turned the deserted corner into my corridor and everything went black.

9
That Hurt

Whoa. Dizzy. Feel sick. Buzzing noise. Faint muttering. Can't make it out. It's dark but there's a light floating around. Maybe if I keep my eyes closed, it'll all go away.

"He's waking up."

"Do we need the water?"

"Only if he won't open his eyes."

I knew these facts: Someone hit me over the head. I lost consciousness. I assumed I'd been moved. The voices I heard did not sound dangerous. But that was nothing to go by.

A hand slapped my cheek. I groaned and rolled my head from side to side. I discovered I was on a cold floor.

"Wake up," was yelled at a level that made my body jolt. I opened my eyes but everything was blurred. I closed them again.

"Get the water."

It didn't sound like the decontamination process again, but I wasn't taking any chances. I opened my eyes. I stretched my eyelids as far as I could. I blinked repeatedly until my vision began to clear.

Shit! It had been one hell of a long day!

I concentrated on the face in front of me and saw the familiar grey hue and stringy hair of a "Remnant." Yes, it was an awful term, but as someone had smashed me over the head, I felt it was deserved.

"Detective Track, we need your help."

"Bloody funny way of getting it," I slurred as a bright

light illuminated the room and seared my retinas. I squeezed my eyes shut. Someone said,

"Turn it off." It went dark. I think I groaned. My head hurt.

"Going to be sick," I said as I turned my head.

"Way to go, Vibe." I assumed Vibe was responsible for my headache.

"Nope, not gonna be sick," I decided I'd rather not lose my dinner.

"Help him up." With a lack of finesse, I was hoisted onto my feet and dumped into a chair. A wall light was switched on, giving a mercifully dull glow throughout the room. "Where am I?" I asked, "and where's my dog?" That last question was probably a little more emphatic than needed when enquiring about a fake pet.

"Your dog is fine. You're in a side room off the COC."

I snorted. The bloody COC. So that's where I'd finally ended up. What was it going to be? Embroidery or pot making? Or how to develop a clanging headache? "Why am I here?" I could focus at last. I was in a small room with about eight different Remnants. Yes, I was still calling them by the hated title. Respect needed to be earned and the lump on my head zeroed their share.

"Detective Track, my name is Mickley." It was the stringy-haired, grey-faced person who had been leaning over me. Now I could see better, it was difficult to pin a gender on the one named Mickley. "We need your help," Mickley repeated.

"And as I said, you've got a bloody funny way of going about it," I winced at the pain in my head.

"I'm sorry. We have been waiting for you to arrive. You appeared to need more… encouragement." Mickley saw me look at the security system.

"It's switched off. No-one is on their way. All we ask is you hear us out. Then if you're convinced you can't help, you leave and you'll never hear from us again."

There was shuffling from the other Remnants in the

room when Mickley said the last sentence.

"You do realise I am no longer a detective. I'm out of commission for three months. Even after that, it's unlikely they'll let me back in."

"We know. An Authority Four detective would be no use to us. The Authority is no use to us."

I felt a wave of nausea hit again and muttered the word "water." I was handed a glass and took a sip, spilling some with shaky hands. "OK, what's going on?" I asked.

Mickley grabbed a chair and straddled it backwards, leaning their hands against the seat back. I still wasn't sure I could pin a male or female gender on Mickley, so I went with neutral. "Our families are going missing."

I groaned before Mickley could say anything else.

"This has already been investigated. Family members were recorded as off-station."

"That's not true," came from a new voice.

Mickley raised a hand to silence the individual. "We do not believe that is true. Even if all the missing family members had left the station, don't you think at least one of them would have sent a message back?"

"I'm listening. What's your theory?"

"We don't have a theory. We have interesting facts. Fourteen of us have supposedly left the station with not one word to our families. Only those of us with prosthetics, your so-called 'Remnants' have gone missing."

"Remnant is not my term. I happen to hate it. Until what's his name-Vibe here cracked me over the head to get me here. You could have asked."

"We tried. Remember the woman at your apartment?"

"Olivian? All too well," I replied.

"She was supposed to persuade you we needed your help. Your care and consideration with our limb maintenance have been noted over the years."

"So much so, you felt the need to inflict a head injury on me," I hissed.

"I have already apologised for Vibe's over-enthusiasm."

I snorted at the terminology. "So, fourteen amputees who use artificial limbs have gone missing. No-one knows where and no-one had heard anything from any of them?" I asked.

"Correct."

"And when all this was reported to the Authority, the cases were closed with an assumption everyone had merely left the station."

"Correct."

"Apart from the issue of no contact, what convinces you they haven't left the station?"

Mickley held a hand out and another Remnant-I was still angry-handed over a device. "This," Mickley said, and handed it to me.

"I don't know what I'm looking at," I said.

"This is a high-end tracking device used in conjunction with high-end prosthetics. One of us was allocated a high-tech prosthesis, no doubt by mistake. It's the type used by VIPs who want to be trackable by their security team but who do not want an implant in their flesh."

"That never made any sense to me. You could just leave the limb somewhere and ditch the tracker," I mused, "OK, and?" My vision blurred again and my head felt worse.

"Look at where it says the prosthesis is."

I squinted at the screen, convinced it would be a more efficient use of time to just tell me. I frowned, "That level doesn't exist. At least not on any plans I've seen of the station."

"Exactly. The prosthesis is still on the station in an unknown part of the structure. Where is the human who is supposed to be attached to it?" Mickley asked.

I looked at the people in the room expectantly. It took my addled brain a while to realise it was a genuine question. "OK, so, what do you think is happening to them?"

The enthusiastic voice called out, "They're taking us."

Mickley raised a hand again. "We have tried to get down to the area where the prosthesis is but access to it appears to be via a ladder unless you have clearance for the lifts."

Mickley waved a hand around the room. "As you can see by the number of missing limbs, we're not perfectly equipped to make the descent."

I thought about mentioning my bum knee. It also wouldn't get me down there, but at least I had a knee, so I held my tongue.

"Are there any other trackable prosthetics down there?" I asked.

Mickley shook the stringy head of hair on their shoulders.

"But you followed protocol and entered the serial numbers into the system, right?" I asked.

"Yes. On that device is a full list of who has gone missing and the corresponding serial numbers of their artificial limbs. If you find any other matching numbers down there, you'll know we're right."

"I haven't agreed to help you yet."

Mickley stood and knocked the chair onto the floor in the process. The raised voice surprised me, "You are our only hope. The Authority denies there is a problem."

I raised my hands for quiet. "OK, I'll agree to look into it for you if you tell me the truth."

The room fell silent, so I continued, "Two questions: did any of you follow me today?" I looked around the room and saw confusion and blank faces. "Second question: have any of you hacked into the system to send me messages today?" Again, I surveyed the room but came up blank.

"Whatever has happened to you today, wasn't us," Mickley said.

"Until you smashed me over the head," I said.

Mickley stared back at me. I wasn't getting another apology.

"OK, I'll look into it. But you must realise, I have no resources, no backup and no clearance to any Authority systems."

The enthusiastic one across the room let out a whoop, and I raised my eyebrows and instantly regretted the movement as it brought another wave of nausea. "This is not going to be a quick operation. I need a few days to heal and a few more to plan. And I need my dog."

Banyon was returned to me and we left the side room of the COC. As we walked across the main area, my eyes were drawn to the large painting on the wall. Jarner had finished it just before the deployment that killed him. As much as I admired and loved his incredible talent, I couldn't bear to have the painting near me at home. It was a sharp blade of a reminder of who I had lost. I had donated it to the COC on the understanding it would not be sold or given away and that I could claim it back whenever I wanted. Maybe that was the real reason I avoided the COC at all costs.

Mickley followed me towards the door. "Would you like Vibe to escort you home?"

I'm not sure if it was a serious or sarcastic question. Were they making a jibe at how easy it was to over-power me or was it a serious concern?

I looked at the large man who went by the name of Vibe and uttered a gruff, "I'll manage."

I stood outside the COC for a few seconds. Unsteady on my feet, the waves of nausea came and went. I staggered towards the lifts and the lair of the late-night medics.

***

I groaned when I entered the medical centre. The lights were set on supernova.

"Have you reported this to the Authority?" the doctor asked.

I refrained from shaking my head, "They have closed the case of a woman who died outside my apartment and a break-in at my apartment. Do you really think they'd be interested in one of their own being cracked over the head?"

"Fair point," the young doctor said. His healthy glow proved he was untouched by Si-Cross Four's biological event.

"I've not seen you before. Have you just arrived?" I asked.

"Been here a couple of months," he said, "Right, I don't

think you've suffered a concussion. You're suffering from the effects of decontamination and the follow-up treatments. I assume you are not drinking alcohol whilst taking the pills you were given?" he asked.

"I assume that would be bad?" I said.

"It will delay your recovery."

I thought for a second. I needed an answer, but I didn't want anything on my medical record.

"Hypothetically," I began, "would any of this cause hallucinations?" I asked.

"No, why, are you experiencing hallucinations? It's important you tell me if you are."

"No, I'm not. Don't worry. I know exactly what's going on," I lied, "It's not medical."

He gave me a suitably dubious look, "There's nothing else medically to do. You need to rest. Go home. Sleep. Your head injury is superficial. There is no sign of swelling and all of your symptoms are due to the interaction of alcohol and medication."

"Noted, thank you. I didn't realise." *Just plain stupid, more like.*

A groan from a patient I hadn't noticed interrupted my thoughts. He was restrained on a bed and appeared to be just coming around. It had been a while since I'd seen someone with *that look*. "Is that an Abyss overdose?" I asked.

The doctor paused, probably contemplating ethics. He rapped his knuckles on the table next to him before continuing, "We have seen a rising number of Abyss overdoses in the last year."

"I thought we managed to stamp out that narcotic years ago," I said as I stared at the patient who was having a worse night than I was.

"We did. But just recently someone has managed to synthesise a new version that is as dangerous as the original. No-one seems to know how or where it came from."

"I'm not even sure it's on our radar." I didn't continue, there didn't seem a point. It could disappear again before I could reclaim my uniform.

"It will be soon," he countered, "I've already submitted the relevant reports."

I thanked the doctor and told myself it was out of my hands.

***

I left the medical suite and wandered slowly home, reassured that there hadn't been any real damage to my head. I leant on the wall in the lift before stumbling out when I reached my floor. I stopped several times to allow the station to stop spinning around me. Finally, I made it through my front door. Banyon, who hadn't left my side since the doctor's examination, ran to his bed and fell into charging mode.

I saw a flashing light on my wall comms. It was from Wicklow. Two words, "Be careful."

10
Rough Night

"Be careful." I didn't know whether to laugh or not. I'd attempted the 'careful' thing that day and still spent some of it unconscious. I hadn't even done anything. I assumed from the warning, Wicklow somehow had an idea of what was going on. It wasn't something she usually said to me.

I groaned loudly. Even my aches ached. I got as far as reaching for my post-decontamination tablets. I crunched them down and fell into the armchair. I had every intention of making it into bed. My body had other ideas.

My dreams that night were a jumble of reality and fantasy. I saw Jarner's picture, full of its vibrant colours and picturesque landscape. In the middle of the picture, I saw Jarner being torn to shreds by bullets. Again, his body danced to the macabre music of flying projectiles. This time he grinned with blood dripping from the corners of his mouth and uttered the word 'soon.' What did that mean? I'd join him soon, or I'd find out what happened to him soon? Did I care which?

The dream changed. I was back in the place we had nicknamed 'Nartern Eleven.' We weren't supposed to be there. It was reserved for the VIPs we most certainly were not. We were in the cave we'd found. The natural rock was covered with plant life which possessed a luminescence and a glow we could see by. We'd found a corner we could rest in, devoid of people and overlooking the internal waterfall. It was unbelievably peaceful.

Nartern Eleven exploded. Glowing rock and plant life

flew towards me. Jarner disappeared from the dream. I ducked from the rock as it flew straight at me. Ethan's arm scurried across mid-air with its fingers wriggling as if walking along a surface. It slowed down as it reached me. I caught it. The arm struggled free and began beating my head in a rhythmical pattern. It sounded hollow, like something hitting a large surface. The arm started shouting.

"Track! Track!"

The thumping continued to clang. The arm muttered something just out of my hearing range. It continued to hit me on the head. I could hear a cat noise. The cat noise pulled at my trouser leg. More voices, too muffled to make out, reached my ears.

Ethan's fist came directly towards my face. Instead of passing out with its impact, I awoke. The room swam for a few seconds before I gained control over my senses. The cat noise was still pulling at my trouser leg. "OK, boy," I muttered to my beleaguered dog, "OK, I'm awake."

More muffled voices from what I determined was beyond my front door. I heaved myself out of my chair and forgot I had a bum knee. I growled under my breath as Banyon hissed in sympathy beside me. My attempt to call, "I'm coming," was lost in my pre-caffeinated state. I reached the door and hit the open switch. The muffled voices obtained clarity.

"I have more concern for my colleague than I do for your constant noise complaints. Why don't you move if you don't like it here?"

"How dare you! I do not see why my wife and I should be uprooted because you and your Authority Four colleague have no idea how to conduct yourselves."

"As I've explained, Detective Track is recovering from a medical event and I'm more concerned about his welfare. If you were any kind of worthy neighbour or human, you would be too."

"Coffee?" I asked, interrupting Laiten's argument with my neighbour. I glared at the latter and said, "Not you." I wasn't in the mood to extend my hospitality to someone with my neighbour's level of humanity. My laundry chute showed more consideration! I left them to it and walked towards the kitchen. My knee chip was finally cooperating, and I could walk a little better. I heard the door close behind me.

"Here, sit down. I'll get the coffee." Laiten strode past me.

I fell into the chair sounding like an old man again as the slightly younger one made himself busy in my kitchen area.

"Rough night?" he asked, "I was knocking for ages again." I was grateful for his concerns but didn't necessarily require him to be my therapist. Banyon hissed around Laiten's legs as I replied,

"Must be the meds. Couldn't wake up. He's after his bone. Top drawer, right-hand side."

Being a robot, Banyon didn't eat. I had developed a "breakfast" routine of throwing him a bone to play with on the mornings I remembered. Just as well he didn't require food at regular intervals.

Laiten was visibly amused as Banyon hissed and took his bone back to his bed. "When are you going to fix his voice?" Laiten asked.

"After coffee," I said, remembering the module in my trouser pocket. I removed the item and set it on the table in front of me. It was hours later, and I could still taste the crunched tablets from last night. I only had two left. They were going down with coffee.

Bags I hadn't noticed Laiten carrying appeared on the table in front of me.

"Lena been baking again?" I asked.

Laiten shook his head. "Leftover cake from last night. She's kept some back but sent me with a piece each."

Why not, I thought, my mouth already tastes like a fetid pit. Everything tasted better with coffee. Except oranges, I mused.

Coffee was placed on the table in front of me. I reached

for it and my pills. I sat for a few minutes awaiting the miracle that is caffeine to take effect.

When I could focus better on the tasks ahead, I called, "Here Banyon," and my dog left his fake bone behind to stand at my side. I picked him up and reached over for the module, groaning with effort to Laiten's amusement.

"Wait until you're old," I said. He laughed and shook his head.

"Right, you fiddly bugger. Let's see if I can switch the module without disassembling you," I said.

"Need a hand?" Laiten asked.

"Maybe, nope, got it," I replied.

"Banyon, bark," I instructed, "Oh shit," I said as Banyon barked and growled with the full force of an attack dog.

"That is a huge voice for such a small dog," Laiten said after almost spraying me with coffee.

"Definitely need to keep his volume down," I said.

"Mr and Mrs Plumer will not be impressed," Laiten said. I gave him a blank look. "Your neighbours?"

I nodded in recognition as I adjusted Banyon's volume.

"You didn't know their names?" he asked.

"I must have done. They've started enough noise reports about me. Must have slipped my mind," I said through a mouthful of drying cake. I drank more coffee to compensate. "Tell me about the investigation into Olivian's murder?"

"There isn't one, it's closed."

"You know that's bullshit, right?"

Laiten nodded, "The order came down from higher than Authority Four. Beynard had no choice."

"And my break-in and the intruder?"

"Same. The official line is that the break-in was the decontamination process. The intruder was a chance encounter with a drug addict who has since left the station. They couldn't dismiss it completely because of the noise complaint from Mr Plumer. If he hadn't made that complaint, it would have gone down as a figment of your imagination.”

I was too tired to throw anything or make a fuss. “So apart from feeding me yesterday’s dessert, why are you here?” I asked.

“To check on you and find out what you intend to do with Banyon’s eye. I’m intrigued.”

“I’m fine, I think, amazingly. And the eye is with a friend.”

“And the bruise on your forehead? That wasn’t there last night when you left our place,” he enquired.

I reached a hand to my head. I hadn’t even noticed I had any visible signs at the front of my head. I thought the impact was around the back. But then I was unconscious, anything could have happened. I poured more coffee from my ancient pot and began to explain the rest of my evening to Laiten.

“So, how the hell are you going to get down there undetected?” Laiten asked as he looked at the station plans and the area the false leg was supposed to reside.

“I have no idea,” I said deliberately. “First things first,” I said getting up, “I’d like to visit Shifton and see how she’s getting on with the eye.”

“May I make a suggestion?” Laiten asked. I looked at him expectantly. “Have a shower first.”

I wrinkled my nose and discovered his advice was sound. Once in the bedroom, I let out a loud yelp of alarm. Laiten rushed in, hand on gun ready to act. “What?” he asked, looking around and failing to see anything of note.

“Have you any idea how early it is?” I asked with wide eyes, pointing at my clock.

Laiten’s face was blank. “I pulled the day shift and wanted to check on you before work.”

“No wonder Mr Friendly Incarnate threw a fit at the racket you made at my door. Some people would call it the middle of the night.”

Laiten shrugged and his hand left the top of his weapon. “If you hurry up, I can go with you to see your tamed tech.”

"She would not appreciate you calling her anything like *tamed*."

I pulled my shirt over my head. My movement was better than the day before and the cream had healed my back enough to submit it to a shower of non-sterile water. You'd have been forgiven believing the noise that escaped my lips was due to something other than hot, soothing water cascading onto my skin. I could just see the look of amusement on Laiten's face in the other room.

Clean at last, and dressed in new civilian garb, I strapped my weapon to my side and pulled on my boots. I contemplated locking Banyon in the cupboard again but somehow couldn't bring myself to go through with it. Getting a grip, any day now…

We left the apartment and headed in different directions. When I realised he wasn't by my side, I turned and caught Laiten up. He was right, the service lifts would be less busy now we were coming up on the early shift start time.

I hit the button for Shifton's level but refused to look at the screen. When I did follow Laiten's gaze, all I saw were numbers. No slow-moving letters of a cryptic message. Maybe I had imagined them.

"I'm impressed," I said, as we entered Shifton's rooms, "you fixed the camera." Then I saw her. Black eye, dried blood on the side of her head and cuts on her bare arms. "What the hell happened?" I asked.

She pointed to the dead body of a man, face down on the floor behind her. "Meet the other guy," she said with a sigh.

Laiten checked for a pulse and confirmed, "He's dead. I'll call it in."

"Wait," I said, "Shif, what happened?"

She sat on her chair, more slumped than I was used to seeing. Her workshop had only been partially recovered from the obvious disturbance of last night.

"After you left last night, someone else banged on the door. I was tired and not concentrating. I thought you'd come back. I opened the door without thinking. I suspected it wasn't a social call–face mask and everything." She threw me the mask.

"Have you run him through the system?" Laiten asked.

"What, the system I'm not supposed to have access to?" Shifton countered. "Yeah," she trailed off.

"Could it be the intruder you saw at your apartment the other night?" Laiten asked me, cutting Shifton's answer short.

"No, this guy is smaller. The intruder was more your build. Turn him over and I'll see if I recognise him."

Before anyone could move a screen came to life. Shifton turned to the controls.

"This isn't great quality," Shifton said, "Given the angle Banyon's eye was recording your first break in, about all I can get is height and build of the individual. But if I compare him to the guy on the floor and run the comparison through this," she pressed buttons. "The dead guy could be the one who ransacked your apartment the other night.

"Roll him over," I said again.

"No need," Shifton said. She stared me straight in the eye and I knew to brace myself for whatever was coming.

"It's your partner, Hegland."

11
Hegland. Why?

My initial reaction was to ignore Shifton's protests and turn over the body on her workshop floor. Despite confirmation from the system, it was my supposedly undercover partner, Hegland, I needed to see for myself.

What I saw was the reason few people worried about Shifton. Hegland's face was unrecognisable. I don't know what she had used to cave in his face, but there weren't corresponding injuries on her knuckles.

"I'm sorry, Track. I had no choice. He came at me with this." She handed me a weapon I had never seen before. "Careful, I don't know how it works," she said.

Laiten backed away from the end I was inadvertently pointing at him. "Track put it down on the floor and let me disarm it," he instructed.

"You know what this is?" I asked.

"I've seen one before."

I laid it down on the floor and stepped away. Laiten stepped in and waved a hand slowly over the length of the short pole. A switch raised from the surface. He turned it and nothing appeared to happen. "It's safe," he announced.

"Are you sure?" Shifton asked.

Laiten nodded. "Not many around. I think it's still in the prototype stage. Lethal in the wrong hands," he half smiled apologetically to Shifton who had confirmed his statement during the night.

"I had no idea what it could do." She slumped forward onto the desk and dropped her head into her hands. Despite being a lethal weapon herself, she once told me she'd never killed anyone.

"Shif," I began, "this was nothing more than self-defence. You had no choice. I looked around the workshop and saw Shifton's capybara robot had suffered the same fate as Hegland's face. I'd help Shifton rebuild the robot when we'd dealt with the soon to be decomposing remains detracting from the ambience of the workshop.

"Look, Track, I need to get to work soon. We need to call this in. It was self-defence," Laiten began.

I shook my head and interrupted. "No, I need Hegland alive for a while."

Shifton lifted her head and threw me a quizzical look. "He's been dead for hours," she said.

"What I mean is, I need his identity to be kept alive. Can you turn me into Hegland on the system and ramp up his clearance to get me into this area?" I took out Mickley's device and told her what I knew. She looked at the secret part of the station no-one seemed to know about.

"What? Research Division?" Laiten and I exchanged a look. Shifton continued, "Well, you two have no need to know about it. We've all done a stint down there at one stage or another." She waved a hand around the workshop indicating the existence of multiple idle workstations.

The inaction of shock wore off. "Are they going to be in soon?" I asked.

Shifton shook her head. "I asked them not to. Said I'd cover. Spun them a line about a Tapinica spill. Told them I'd clean it up and let them know when they could come in."

"What the hell is Tapinica?" I asked, conscious of so many things in the room with the potential to kill me.

"Perfectly safe. Very sticky. A complete bitch to remove. Told them I'd only dropped it on the floor." She looked exhausted.

"We still need to stash the body," Laiten was getting impatient, "and that weapon," he added.

"Got it," Shifton began. She tapped instructions into a

wall console. An inner glass door opened. A large metal box arrived in the airlock. The inner door closed and a fog of gases jetted over the box before the door to our area opened.

Shifton opened the box. It was a secure storage vessel for just about anything of value.

"I wonder if one has been used for this purpose before," I said as Shifton and I hefted Hegland's body into the box. I retrieved any credentials I could find on his body and handed them to Shifton as Laiten carefully laid the weapon next to my dead partner.

Shifton closed the box and the outer door. More jets of gas enveloped the box before the inner door opened and the room swallowed Hegland's encased body.

"Make plans," Laiten said, "do nothing until I get off shift. You need backup," he said as he left the room.

I looked around the room at anything that may require turning up the right way, but much like my desk, I suspected the workshop was almost ship-shape.

Shifton assessed the damage to her capybara with a defeated air about her. I pulled a chair upright and pushed a free-standing cabinet back in place before joining her on the floor.

"Can you fix her?" I asked.

"Probably. But I won't be able to hide the nature of the damage from the others." She looked at me with sunken, red-rimmed eyes.

"Before you call the others back in," I said, "go through what happened last night."

"Track, I swear to you, it was self-defence," she pleaded.

I ventured a hand onto her back and did not have my arm ripped out of its socket. I've already told you, Shifton was potentially lethal. Any sensible person would exercise caution. "I don't doubt it for a second. But it will do you good to tell me exactly what happened after he came in." At that moment I couldn't name the dead body as my partner, Hegland. That would have made it too real. I'd known him for years and now…

"He didn't see me at first. I remotely opened the door, assuming it was you and was over there," she pointed to a colleague's high-walled area containing various technology. "I came around the corner. He saw me, raised the weapon at me and demanded I gave him the eyeball. He couldn't see it on the desk, it was obscured. I told him he couldn't have it and he opened fire on Rosie," she pulled the giant rodent towards her. Apart from occasional, convenient neglect, we all treated our fake pets like real ones.

"I'll help you fix her," I said. Shifton suddenly looked like a small child which made her next words all the more chilling.

Through gritted teeth, she began, "I just saw red. He pointed that weapon towards me and I rushed him. I didn't give a shit if it went off and killed me. We struggled with it. His mask got pulled off. I got thrown into some furniture and chairs went flying. Eventually, I pulled the thing away from him, but something happened to it and as I was holding it, the weapon vibrated. He knew what was coming even though it happened so quickly. The look on his face before the weapon discharged-I don't think I'll ever forget it."

"It's OK," I lied. Shifton would never be the same again. I braved putting my arm around her shoulders, survived, and was surprised Shifton curled into my arms. We sat there for a few seconds on the floor. A mangled robot capybara next to us and the body of my partner in the secure storage next door. I guess it proved one thing, no matter how tough a person's exterior, inside you'll probably find a human as confused and scared as anyone else. Shifton moved.

"Right, enough," she said. The change back to her normal personality had the same effect as a bucket of cold water being tipped over my head. She stood and offered me a hand up, which I took. "Sit down and roll up your trouser leg."

"This isn't one of those funny clubs, is it?" I asked. I was deflecting. Part of me was still in shock. Part of me wanted to yell, *how could you?* Part of me completely understood my partner pulled a 'him or her' situation on Shifton. Maybe I'd accept it if I understood why.

Shifton looked at me and waited for me to comply with her instructions. I pulled my trouser leg up. She frowned. "Wrong leg," she said.

"Sorry, thought you just wanted to admire the good one," I said when I realised she was attempting maintenance on the chip in my bad knee. Shifton's usual humour had taken a hit since her actions of the previous night. Hardly surprising.

She took in a breath as she saw my knee. "Swollen. You should put ice on this every day."

"Yeah, about that," I didn't need to continue. She knew I hadn't heeded her warnings.

"I'll do my best," she said. I thanked her and sat back while she attached the-whatever it was-to my knee. I closed my eyes to think.

What had Hegland wanted with Banyon's eye? Or was it something else he was looking for and took the eye because he recognised it as a camera? I didn't even know that. It was no good, I was so tired my levels of concentration had dropped to where I could successfully throw Banyon a ball if I really put effort into it.

My chin hit my chest and woke me up. "Sorry," I mumbled.

"It's OK. What are we going to tell the others about Rosie?"

"Huh?" my mind ran through people and names and drew a blank.

"My capybara?" Shifton snapped.

"Yes, sorry, I forgot that was what you called her. They'll know something happened as soon as they see her. Can you trust them?"

"Yes, of course."

"You sure?" I asked. Shifton gave me a look instructing me not to take the question any further.

"OK. How many are currently working here?"

"Just the three of us. But Lax picked up a cushy job on Si-Cross Six. Only Mothball is due in today."

I never got to the bottom of why he was called Mothball but I had worked with him in the past. "How about this? Tell Mothball the truth. See if he can help adapt the ID to get me into that Research Division." I still couldn't bring myself to use Hegland's name in conversation.

Shifton thought for a second. "I can trust him and he would be useful to have on board."

"Good." I looked at the gadgetry attached to my knee. It was usually at about this time that Shifton's chip calibrations or whatever she did, finished. I think she put the coloured lights on the device to give me an impression it was doing something. They weren't there originally and having a visual countdown seemed to keep me quiet. Devious woman. Clever, but devious. The last light went out.

"All done," she announced. "You should be able to move around easier and your knee tech should be quicker to respond."

"Thanks," I said to a dismissive wave of Shifton's hand. Assuming I had been dismissed, I pulled myself out of the chair intending to test my knee on the way to the door.

"Hang-on!"

I looked around. Shifton was staring intently at a screen whilst waving for me to approach. Before I could ask why she said, "There's something else on the eyeball. It's another file. An audio-visual file by the look of it. Corrupt of course, and it'll take hours to clean up like the last one. I'll do my best."

I was about to thank her when the door opened. Shifton visibly blanched. I reached for my weapon.

Mothball waited until the door closed behind him and asked, "What's up?" He limped in and took a seat while Shifton explained the basics of what we were dealing with.

Mothball was one of the ultra-lucky survivors. How he survived the biological event, people could only speculate. He had died no fewer than five times on three separate days.

They had taken both his legs above the knees to save his life. He took one of the longest times to recover. You could say they mothballed him at the time if he hadn't already arrived at the station with the name. Mothball was a bit of a legend in these parts.

Shifton had reached the end of her narrative. A suitably shocked Mothball turned to face me. He'd given up using makeup to appear more… not dead. His pallor was such that the undertakers of Lesterg would be appalled.

"Can you help?" I asked.

"Sure, I'll give it a shot," he replied.

"Have you noticed anything unusual recently?" I asked. Mothball shook his head.

"You need to keep your eyes open. Until I know more, we need to assume anyone using artificial limbs is a target for whatever the hell is going on."

"Have you any idea?" Shifton asked.

"Other than whoever is behind this needs to be ejected, suit-less from the nearest air-lock? No. Shif you need to get some rest. I need you two to look out for each other." I walked towards the door. "Oh wow, that is a lot better thanks," I said, referring to my knee.

"I'll sleep here while Moth works on the ID and access."

"OK good." I guess she meant capybara corner where she kept a sofa and some blankets.

"I'm going back to my apartment. I still need more rest before I do anything. That was a bloody early call I had this morning. Let me know when you've cracked the ID, the access and the file. And now you've fixed it, use the security camera."

***

I made good time back to my apartment. It was only after Shifton adjusted the tech in my knee I realised how bad it got. I was lucky it still worked. It was a temporary fix long past its recycle date.

The corridors were sparsely populated. I had no sense that anyone was following me and none of the screens tried to remind me about Nartern Eleven.

I closed the door to my apartment and leant back against it. Sliding down towards the floor with my head in my hands, I cried for my best friend. Why the hell had Hegland gone in masked. Why had he attacked and why did he want Banyon's eye?

12
Fixing Day

I couldn't tell you how long I was on the floor by my front door crying. It wasn't something I was accustomed to. I'd held it together when I'd been told about Jarner's death. Maybe that's why I was in a state now. At some point, Banyon ran over and I found myself rubbing the robot's ears and sobbing over the demise of my best friend. I was a bloody mess.

When I'd finally given up on my bout of self-pity, I dragged myself to my feet and limped towards my sink. After a few steps, I remembered my knee had received maintenance and found I could walk with hardly a limp. If I found out Shifton's calibrations were placebos, I'd take her on. I'd be knocked out in three seconds, but I'd be seething while unconscious.

Water spluttered from the tap and I doused my face, killed the water and dried my face on the kitchen towel. Yeah, I can hear your disapproval, watch me not care!

I had no plans for the day other than making plans. To be honest, I had very few ideas about those. I was stuck until I knew I could get past the lift security and down into Research Division. It would have been easier if one of the techs was currently working there, I wouldn't have risked any of them, but I'd have taken their access.

I made a list.

-Fix Banyon's patchy fur.

-Fix Ethan's peeling face.

Well, that was relevant to the mission.

I had no appetite for the infiltration of Research. Even if I got in, I'm not sure what Mickley expected me to achieve. I could film it for evidence. I remembered a time when that would have helped.

"Nope, this is crap," I said out loud. I was too on edge to sleep and not quite desperate enough for a nail covering course at the COC. I had a comical vision of Jarner with all his artistic ability, sitting opposite a Remn… a bio-event survivor passing the time of day while he constructed intricate patterns to cover their grey and decaying fingernails. A far cry from the battlefield, but he would have been good at that. I laughed out loud.

Enough. I was about to convince myself I could eat something. "Later Banyon," I said as I checked my pockets for civilian station accreditation. I still had my weapon. As a last resort, I checked the case I took with me on occasions like these and threw it on my back. There was only one thing I could eat at any time of day. It was heavy, it was fried, it was sickly sweet, you could get it in a multitude of flavours and it was called Schuror. It possessed absolutely no nutritional value whatsoever and was, therefore, a banned item the authority had long since given up policing.

***

"Track, good to see you," Carrie said.

"Ignore me, I'm not here to arrest you," I joked, "I'll take four please."

"Someone's hungry," she said, removing my future heart attack from the fryer to drain. I looked at the coatings available. There was always something new.

"I'll have one of whatever that is," I said pointing to the vat of luminescent green, "and, ugh, I dunno, the rest in the usual, thanks," I muttered something about comfort food rather than hunger. Lifting my thumb to pay, Carrie interrupted me.

"Other one," she sang to me. I nodded.

"It wouldn't do to pay for it with my approved Authority account," I said. Yes, I had one thumb for supplies approved by the Authority and the other one linked to an account the Authority didn't directly pay and take credit from. We all did. Some of us had to use retinas where digits were absent. No-one knew for sure that the Authority interrogated our official accounts, but we were paranoid enough to use other means. Carrie widened her eyes and shook her head with a playful grin. I lifted my other thumb and allowed my unofficial credit channel to pay for my arterial blockage.

"Eat the green one first," she said, "you'll need the sweet ones afterwards." She handed me my delicious plate of elongated fried stodge and the green one which I was now having doubts about.

It's not that Carrie's illicit Schuror outlet was seedy, it was more like the level of optimism declined with the arrival of its clientele. I looked around at the sullen, depressed and long past hope. This was the side of Si-Cross Four the Authority kept hidden at all costs. We relied on the success of business meetings and the income they brought. Business people were more likely to sign deals if they weren't surrounded by those who had already given up on life.

As I raised the long green cylinder to my mouth, I was aware of almost all the outlet's eyes on me. My eyes moved from left to right and all conversation stopped as I bit into whatever Green Glamour was.

What happened next was not glamorous. As I swallowed the white flame that irrevocably eroded my throat on its way down, my head detached and spun in mid-air whilst sirens sounded and flames issued from my ears. Or that was how it felt. Not that I could see through the tears running down my face, but in case someone was watching, I took a breath of cooling recycled air and managed to croak, "Mmmm, really good," before a hole appeared in my throat and I died completely.

"Bit hot?" Carrie asked. I looked to where I thought she was standing. What with the sweat and the tears I couldn't be sure, it was not like I had use of my vision.

"Meh," I managed, waving a shaky hand in dismissal.

"Here," she said. I could feel the offending weapon being pulled from my hands and a cup of something taking its place. "Drink," she said. First, I was still blind from tears, second, I was dead anyway, so what the hell. I drank. I don't know what I drank, but I didn't die any further.

"You can do my feet as well if you like," I spluttered as I felt Carrie wipe the remains of the toxin from my fingers. When my vision returned and my voice dropped back to a level lower than a shriek, I asked, "What was that?"

"Something I'm not buying again. If you can't take it, no-one else on the station will," she shook her head and replaced the nuclear strip of Schuror with one more suited for a species not trying to emulate a volcano. "Oh no," she said, "I've got to go."

I watched her return to the counter and apologise to a carer and the little girl I'd seen in the lift earlier.

"I knew I shouldn't have let you try it, I'm so sorry," Carrie turned to the small child and asked, "Are you OK honey?"

"Please?" the little girl pleaded with the man she was with. He threw his hands up in disbelief,

"OK, another green one please."

Speechless, Carrie dipped a fresh strip in the same vat that had nearly killed me.

"Thank you so much," the little girl said with a beaming smile on her face as she bounced as best she could on her legs towards a table.

Collectively, we swivelled. None of us breathed as this tiny child took a large bite of fried fire… and grinned.

"So yummy," she said after she swallowed. The man looked around the room, shook his head and shrugged. I stared at Carrie. She returned my disbelieving expression.

"My week just gets weirder," I muttered and coughed again before consuming the rest of my food.

The girl and the man walked past me to leave. I smiled at her. The man behind her stopped abruptly and jogged my table. His hand landed a small distance from my plate. "So sorry," he said.

I waved him off. "Not a problem," I replied as I saw a folded piece of paper he'd left behind.

The rest of the room reverted to their gloomy existence as I picked up the paper and unfolded it. Eight seven four six. My face went blank as I breathed through my exasperation. "Nartern Eleven" was one thing. At least I had a context for that even if I didn't understand the significance of the messages. Eight seven four six was a meaningless combination of digits. Who exactly thinks cryptic messages are a good idea, anyway? I could die before I figured that out. What was I supposed to use? Telepathy? Arsehole. I finished my Schuror and decided the numbers meant nothing and the man dropped it by mistake. I pocketed the paper in case of future revelations.

The members of the room were eyeing me again. I clapped my hands together. "OK," I said, "who needs me to look at something?" I removed my case and set it down beside my stool whilst Carrie cleared away my plate. They knew the drill, I'd help maintain their limbs if I was able. I could not officially receive anything in return as technically I was not helping to maintain Authority property. The people and their limbs were no better than rejects in the eyes of the powers that be. I was also not qualified for anything like this. Taking payment was never an option. These people deserved better, but I was all they had. I didn't like the gratitude. I wasn't their hero. I was just a man with a set of tools and an aptitude for mechanical things.

Small talk was kept to a minimum. They could tell me the problem or ask me to tighten this and loosen that, but I wasn't embarking on deep meaningful conversations with any of them.

I looked in mock anger at the man in the wheelchair. Clearly, the fix I had implemented on his legs a while ago wasn't worth the time I'd put in. I turned them over under the ceiling light. Something caught my eye. It wasn't what I had done last time, but the part I'd replaced the time before.

"Bloody amateur hour," I muttered berating my own work. Lifting my case onto the table, I opened it and rummaged around until I found what I needed. By the time I'd used my fourth tool and added more expletives to my repertoire, I had removed the offending part and replaced it with a better option. I handed them back, and he was wheeled away to the side of the room to be helped onto them. If they were better, he'd leave. If not, he'd join the queue again. And so, the conveyor belt moved on.

"What's this?" I asked of a young woman holding an unfamiliar bottle.

"It's the new liquid we're supposed to use," she replied.

The survivors had been using the same standard lubricant for years. It did its job. The supplier was still in business. The stuff was dirt cheap. I saw no reason for the change. It probably meant nothing. But somehow, I felt uneasy. "Any chance I can swap it for an old one? I've never seen this before. Is it any good?" I asked.

She was taken aback by my sudden urge for conversation and didn't answer until I nodded my head and told her it was OK. "It's not as good as the original. You need to use more of it. We can't order it individually either, we have to pick it up from the mainline stores on sixty-three."

That explanation made my reason for wanting it more acceptable. "Let me swap it. I'll have a friend look at it and make sure they aren't fobbing you off with a watered-down version."

"OK," she said and took one of my two remaining bottles of original machine lube in return for her new one.

I worked my way through my line of mechanical problems. The guy in the wheelchair didn't come back. I assumed his legs were OK, or he'd given up on my inept efforts. I replaced worn out parts. A few of the interiors could have benefited from replacement mouldings and padding for comfort-but I would have needed the sewing course from the COC for that.

The last quiet thanks rang in my ears. I closed my eyes,

not knowing if I'd helped. I hoped I hadn't made anything worse. The stress of the last few days had drastically reduced as it always did when I was attempting to improve things.

Opening my eyes, I looked around and now my work for the day was complete, Carrie brought me a coffee and another strip of Schuror. My reward for helping. As I wouldn't take anything other than leftovers in return for tinkering with artificial limbs, Carrie wouldn't take anything for my post fixing day refreshments. She sat across the table from me.

"That was a lot of people today, Track. You did a huge amount of good."

I waved her off. "Did they buy any?" I asked.

She nodded and took a sip of coffee. "I wish I could offer them something more nutritious, but I'm not allowed those ingredients. Even if I was, I couldn't afford them. I can't even afford to give this stuff away."

"At least they get something when they come here. It's filling, and it's better than nothing." I reassured.

My comms unit lit up. Laiten was summoning me down to meet him, Shif and Mothball.

My therapeutic few hours were over, and the real world had gate-crashed my party.

Dumb bloody world.

13
So, what's the plan?

As I wandered towards the bright lights of Shifton's domain, I didn't feel the usual buzz I experienced after helping the station's neglected. I didn't fix what I could for my own gratification, but it didn't hurt to feel good about myself occasionally. I wasn't feeling it.

On auto-pilot, I turned a corner to be greeted by an outcry. Without thinking about my current employment status, I approached the apartment in question to hear the words, "Maybe it would be best if we spoke inside." It felt like I hadn't heard Wicklow's voice in ages. She tried to usher the couple inside, away from view. I briefly shook my head in annoyance and took two steps before I stopped dead. It was the woman from the lift and the man from Carrie's who left me the note. I had a feeling of dread for the little girl.

"Track," a man's voice called out behind me. Angry at being kept out of the loop because of ridiculous rules, I twisted awkwardly, wrenched my knee and turned towards the man. He leant over Wicklow who gave up trying to handle the taller person back into the apartment. I looked at him. I knew Wicklow would not talk to me. The rules were absolute.

I waited for him to gather his thoughts. He was a mess. His eyes were red. His hair was in disarray, no doubt due to repeatedly running his hands through it. Over his shoulder, I could see the woman sobbing on the sofa, clutching a child's toy. There was no child in sight.

My spine ran cold. I shifted my gaze to the man and clenched my teeth. I would take any announcement from him other than the one I knew he was about to make. "They've taken her. Our little girl. Tamara. She's gone."

Even if I could tell him I heard and understood without Wicklow being compromised, I wouldn't have been able to utter the words. I was livid. All I could do was meet his eyes and nod and hope he understood. Wicklow had positioned herself, so her uniform would only record a video of the couple, not me. The microphone would pick up everything.

"Wicklow will take the case. I am no longer working for Authority Four," I managed. I could hear louder wailing from inside the apartment. Again, I tried to convey a look of "I'm working on it" via my eyes and telepathic powers I did not possess. I have no idea if he understood.

Of course, there was a chance the bubbly little girl had wandered off on her own. I knew deep down this wasn't the case.

As I turned to resume my walk to Laiten and Shifton, I was seething. How dare they? She was a small child in no position to defend herself. If they'd so much as touched a stringy hair on her head, I would end them.

The sounds of wailing diminished as I distanced myself from the apartment. I hammered on the door of my friendly techs as if they were guilty of something. After a few seconds, the door swung open.

"Do you mind?" Shifton asked. Her lips were pursed, and she was not pleased to see me.

"What?" I asked like the idiot I am.

"I really have to explain this to you? I was attacked in here last night. You scared the crap out of me."

"Didn't you see me on the camera?"

"I was asleep. I awoke to you trying to bash the door in while Mothball was looking for weapons to defend ourselves with."

"Sorry," yeah, that was all I had. One pathetic single word. I was taken aback by Shifton being scared shitless by anything.

"For the record, Moth, that cabinet, bottom drawer," Shifton pointed.

Mothball swung himself around on his ill-fitting legs and hobbled over to the cabinet. His legs afforded him more movement than the little girl in the lift who I now knew to be called Tamara. Mothball bent down and opened the drawer before calling out, "Cool. Are they charged?"

"Of course they are. There'd be no point in keeping them if they weren't," she paused, "sorry," she apologised for her tone.

All three of us jumped at more thumping at the door. I found a screen, confirmed my suspicions and said, "Laiten."

As I opened the door to let Laiten in, Shifton muttered, "Right, that's it. I have had enough."

I opened my mouth to say something, but she raised a hand to silence me and my jaw snapped shut. Shifton sat heavily in her chair and manipulated an impressive bank of screens. Laiten opened his mouth, and I gave him the same raised hand treatment. Mothball clearly understood the situation better than we did and remained silent.

"Right," Shifton said in a high, no-nonsense tone. "I have programmed both of you for entry to these rooms. You are to knock three times before scanning and entering. Or at least announce your presence. Understood?"

"Understood."

"Yep."

Laiten and I looked at each other unsure if it was safe to begin a conversation. We looked at Shifton who returned our stare.

"Well? Are we going to stand here gawping, or does anyone have anything useful to say?" she asked. I really had rattled her cage. Or added to anxiety I didn't think she suffered from.

To avoid a verbal free for all, I raised my hand, "Let me go first. You remember the little girl from the lift?" I turned to Laiten who nodded. "Turns out she lives near me," I continued, "She's missing. Now, I have no access to Authority Four systems and there is a possibility she's wandered off. But I suspect with the legs she's using, she wouldn't want to go far on her own. Her father said she'd been taken. Wicklow was about to interview the parents, so I couldn't say anything without compromising both of us with the footage."

Laiten nodded in understanding. "So, what's the plan?" he asked.

I shrugged, "Pilfer ID, break into the lift, go down to Research Division and look around."

"Is that all you've got?" Laiten asked.

"Well until we know what's down there, I have no idea what else to suggest," I countered.

Laiten scratched his head. He was clearly amused at my day's planning effort.

"I pulled up the plans earlier," Shifton began, "I can get you into Research. Track, you're masquerading as…" She paused, struggling to say the name of the man she'd had to kill. She took a breath before continuing, "You've got Hegland's ID. I've adapted it for Research access at the highest level. Laiten, I've had to create a copy of a valid ID belonging to someone who isn't currently on the station so it doesn't appear as a double entry. They get suspicious when someone appears in two places at once. Professor Jane Michaels is the closest match. Unfortunately, she's very well known down there. So try not to get caught. If anyone checks your ID and sees her name, they'll know you're an imposter." She handed us the ID badges and a small handheld device each. "It's thumb and retina scans down there. I've hacked in and changed them over to yours from data I retrieved from the Authority database."

Laiten and I looked at each other.

"Is that easy to do?" I asked.

"No."

I waited for further explanation from Shifton but none was forthcoming. She continued, "These handhelds are prototypes. I've uploaded a map of Research Division to the devices. You'll need these earpieces." Shifton held out her hand and Laiten and I took a small orange bud each and raised it to our ears. "Don't put them in your ears," Shifton called, "chew them."

On any other week, I would have begun considering this to be an elaborate joke. But too much serious crap had taken place. We chewed. Shifton pounced with a gadget in each hand. She pressed one against mine and Laiten's necks. There was a click, a hiss and a yelp as something sharp burrowed into our necks below the ear. "Keep chewing the gum. The action helps the earpiece to bed down."

"Can we carry our IDs in pockets or do you need to insert them anally?" I asked.

"In your dreams," Shifton responded.

"What about the device Mickley gave me?" I asked.

"You won't need it. Everything on it has been uploaded to the new ones, which, as you can see are smaller and lighter."

Shifton sat back down in her chair and Laiten and I sat in the ones Mothball had wheeled over before retreating to the other side of the room. "I'm going to activate your earpieces. Sometimes it stings a little when they are first switched on."

Laiten and I exchanged looks again and waited. Nothing happened. Shifton hit two keys at the same time. I have no idea how Laiten reacted, but I seem to recall screaming like a girl, thrusting my head between my knees and only just managing to refrain from rocking back and forth in the chair. When I finally persuaded my eardrums to climb back inside, I sniffed and wiped my eyes. It was then I realised Laiten had not faired any better.

"Sting a little?" he asked.

"Well, OK, it's intensely unpleasant but hugely useful. At the moment we can only talk among ourselves. The handheld is the transmitter keep it on you at all times. To turn the earpiece on and off, press it."

We stared her down. I wasn't in favour of my brains

leaking out of my nostrils as a result.

"You won't feel it," she insisted.

I took a breath, but before I could man up, Laiten tapped the side of his neck. I followed. A man's voice appeared in my ear.

"You should now be able to hear me," Mothball said from the other side of the room. I was about to move the conversation on when Laiten began speaking to Mothball.

"Seriously, can you hear me?"

"Yes."

"From over here?"

"Yes."

"At this volume?"

"Yes."

"Yes, it's very impressive," I interjected. Shifton raised a hand. The room fell silent.

"You can also switch the earpieces off by turning the transmitter off." Shifton produced her handheld device and brought up a screen to demonstrate how the transmitter worked. Again, I wondered briefly about the joke potential. The transmitter screen had two touch sensitive buttons. One was labelled "on" and the other-yeah, you didn't need that demo either.

"When you get to Research, we'll be able to guide you in case you have your hands full and can't follow the map," she said.

I was about to mention something along the lines of not being threatened by a bunch of scientists until I remembered who I was talking to. Shifton was unique. But for all I knew, science school had a rampant defence skills class added to the curriculum.

"What is the security down there?" I asked.

"Electronic. Everything is behind closed doors. They know we have the skills to hack the system and gain access. But we're employed on a basis of trust."

"This will screw up your career won't it?" I asked the pair. Mothball raised his eyebrows with a look of derision and Shifton said,

"If they're keeping people down there against their will, I won't stand by and do nothing for the sake of my career."

I nodded in agreement. "So, no guards, human or robot, as far as you know?" I asked.

"Not unless the security protocols have changed recently. The only thing I can't do is hack into the video feed down there. They've upgraded the system. You can wear cameras so we can see what you do, but I can't look ahead for you. We're combing through status and security logs to see if there are any updates that may be pertinent, but it's taking longer than expected."

"Understood," I said as I glanced over to Laiten. "Shall we?" I asked. He nodded. "Anything else before we go?" I asked of Shifton and Mothball. They shook their heads. I pulled myself out of my chair and followed Laiten to the door checking the map for directions to the correct lifts.

"This way," Laiten said. I dutifully followed. I must have checked I had my weapon on me three times before we made it to the first security door between us and Research. We reached the first door. I could see the lifts through the window in the door. I scanned. Nothing happened. I heard Laiten mutter something under his breath. We could both see a person who no doubt had approved accreditation approach from the other end of the corridor.

Laiten scanned. Nothing happened. I swore under my breath.

"Is that door playing up again?" the man asked as he reached us.

"Looks like it," I said, smiling like a person who had every right to open the bloody thing.

"Let me try," he said, "ah, there you go. After you. Have a good evening."

"You too," I said pleasantly, "and thank you."

The man followed us through the door and took a right turn. We could see our lifts straight ahead. "Just keep walking," I said under my breath to Laiten. We reached the end. I scanned for the lift. It began to move. The doors opened to reveal an empty metal chamber. I walked in and closed my eyes for a second before turning around and reaching for the button.

"Hold the lift," a young woman ran from a side corridor and joined us before the doors closed.

We had no disguises. I had been all over this station. And there was no way in the world I had not bumped into Research Division personnel outside of their secret laboratories at one time or another. The more people we met, the more likely I was to be discovered. This suddenly felt like a stupid plan.

We stopped. The woman left first. I put one foot outside the lift into Research Division and an alarm sounded.

14
Blindfolded in a Maze

"What do we do?" Laiten asked.

I could barely hear his whisper with the alarm still ringing. In the distance, a person left a room on one side of the corridor and entered a room on the other. There was no urgency to their movement. I stood for a few seconds before the lift doors closed, forcing us to step into this unknown area. The rush of adrenaline coursed through me. Half of me wanted to walk back into the lift and straight into Ethan's 'Ol Bar. I put a pin in it. The other half of me latched onto this mystery before me and knew I was committed right to the end. I tapped the side of my neck.

"Shif, did we cause this alarm?" I waited for a response and expected dead air.

"No, that alarm goes off all the time. Someone probably spilt something. You'll look suspicious just standing there, move."

"What are we expecting to find?" Laiten asked.

"Well," I said in a cheery voice, "I don't know about you, but I'm expecting to open the first door I come to and see more than a dozen missing people waiting to be taken to safety." I turned to Laiten and grinned. His engineered, young face looked back at me and may as well have had *you arse* tattooed on it.

The long corridor was one of the better preserved on the base. Its bright lights could magnify any flaw but I couldn't see any. "This place is immaculate," I muttered. I almost missed a step when the unexpected voice of Mothball appeared in my ears.

"It's not all like that. You're in the front display area. Those rooms are used to show off various merchandise to the highest bidder. You need to go deeper."

I had heard his message but was still reeling from the reality of a voice materialising in my head with no notice. "Does this earpiece have an early warning system or am I going to have a heart-attack every time one of you speaks?"

"You'll get used to it," Shifton said.

We hadn't gone far when a group of men appeared from a side corridor.

"Pretend you're talking," Shifton instructed.

"They'll lock me up."

"Not to me, you idiot, to Laiten." I could sense Shifton's eyes gazing at the ceiling in disbelief. The men were carrying similar screens to ours so I produced mine and started talking to Laiten while pointing at the screen. They took no notice of us and disappeared down another corridor.

"OK, let's speed this venture up, where do we need to go?" I brought the map up on the screen, but it was still new technology I wasn't familiar with, and I may as well have been blindfolded in a maze.

"Go to the end of the corridor and turn left," Shifton said.

My body jolted at her voice and I was glad I'd used the toilet before we left. "I am not going to get used to this earpiece."

"Stop moaning and walk."

"Yes, ma'am."

The pristine white of the first corridor was replaced with a bright orange on the wall to the left. I winced at the garish colour. Laiten didn't appear to be affected by anything.

"Are the rest of them orange or are they colour coded?" I asked.

"Neither, the colours are random," Mothball replied.

"I hope they have blue," I said, "I like blue." Out of the corner of my eye, I could see Laiten's face slowly turn to give me one of those looks that questioned my sanity, intelligence or both. A door opened behind us and at least four people, judging by the number of distinct voices I could hear, entered the glaring orange corridor.

"Hey," a voice called out. I almost staggered. We kept walking. I ran through scenarios of opening random doors and hiding, or worse, running.

"Hey," the voice called again. I thought it would be more suspicious to ignore it a second time, so I looked over my shoulder to see the group turn to the man who called out and heard, "Hey Jinx, sorry, I was in a world of my own, everyone meet Jinx. How are you doing?"

I took two steps with my eyes closed and swallowed. "Where next?" I asked.

"End of the corridor. The last door on the right." Shifton instructed, "you need to scan."

I took a deep breath, my heart was pounding when I turned to Laiten and said, "So, you seem to be annoyingly unaffected by all of this."

"No, no, I'm filled with as much abject terror as I can see pouring off you," he replied.

"Can you two at least try to act like you belong there?" Shifton demanded, "Track, how many times have you been undercover?"

I didn't want to let on Wicklow and others had pulled me out of more near-death experiences than I should have survived. Undercover work had been more Jarner and Wicklow's thing. And the man whose ID I had appropriated. I still couldn't think too deeply about Hegland. We reached the door. I stared at the scanner and waited for the alarm to sound or the door to refuse to open. Click. I glanced at Laiten with an impressed look on my face. Pushing the door open, I stepped into the dark room.

"Lights," I muttered. My eyes widened in surprise when the room lit up. "I was asking where the switch was, didn't expect automation." After the initial glare wore off, we looked around. "This is just a room. It doesn't lead anywhere," I stated.

"There's a drawer on the left… I think the top row, third from the left," Shifton said.

"Got it," I said.

"Beige cylinder?" she asked.

"Yep."

"Great, take it, I'll need that later."

"Why do I get the impression this tube has nothing to do with our current mission?" I asked. Shifton didn't respond, thereby answering my question.

"This is one of the numbers from Mickley's list," Laiten said.

I pocketed the tube and joined him at the far corner of the room to see an artificial arm laid out on a stand with lubrication gunk being drained into a container. "Are our cameras picking this up?" I asked.

"Yes, everything is coming through," Mothball replied.

"Come out of that room, turn to your right and go through the door."

We obeyed and were shocked by what greeted us beyond the door. "It looks like everyone threw up in here," Laiten complained.

"I swear I can smell vomit," I said.

"No, you can't. It is one of the more interesting colour schemes they've used on corridors down there. Hideous isn't it?"

We agreed.

"OK, third door on the left."

Glad to be out of the 'vomidor' I was distracted as we walked through the third door. "Please state the nature of your visit to this artichoke."

"Er, Shif, there's a robot, and he's asking about vegetables," I said.

"Yes, I can hear him. Mothball?"

"Tell him 'it's positively mandibular out there today,'" Mothball instructed.

I repeated the words, and the robot replied, "I'm so

pleased to make your turnips," and stepped aside.

"That conversation did not just happen," I muttered.

"It's Webster, he's harmless. His language module needs fixing but somehow no-one has got around to doing it," Shifton said.

"And the conversation? What happens if you try to walk around him?" I could hear Mothball laughing in the background.

It was Shifton's voice that filled my ears. "He makes a robot version of a crying noise."

"And you know this how?" I asked.

Shifton muttered something I didn't catch and Mothball's laughter grew louder. "Shif can't say the word mandibular, she set him off one day and he cried for hours."

"Yes and then he stopped sobbing and started talking to himself about juicing the limbs of all things." Shifton rattled the words off.

"Why don't you techs power him down until he can be fixed?" I swear I heard a gasp over my earpiece.

"Because he's Webster," Shifton replied. Well, that explained everything.

"OK, moving on, where next?" I asked.

"There's another lift at the end of the corridor."

As we walked towards the lift, Laiten asked, "Are these walls green or grey?"

"Yes," I replied. Laiten reached the lift first and scanned. We performed the dance of all newly acquainted people who found themselves waiting for lifts and looked around us finding nothing to say. Inside the lift, I realised I didn't know which floor to press and looked at the buttons, then Laiten, then the buttons again. "Shifton, do we want praline, caramel, nutty…"

"Toffee," she interrupted, "go to toffee and no, don't ask."

I hit the button marked toffee and waited to wake up from Si-Cross Four's most bizarre dream.

The door opened, and we stepped out into a corridor of

glass-fronted rooms, just as Mothball said, "Oh, shit!"

We waited. I looked around us. Just because I couldn't see surveillance cameras didn't mean they weren't there. We started walking away from the lift and reached the corner of the first room. I heard voices from the room and in my earpiece.

"STOP!" it was Shifton, "Get in the alcove."

We moved.

"OK listen, you need to go down that corridor because it'll take too long to backtrack. I've just found a log entry. The meeting I thought was taking place in two days is in that room tonight. You cannot be seen, these are not friendlies and they might be mixed up in all this. The glass has an opaque patch along the bottom, you'll have to crouch or crawl."

"Are we expecting any other rooms to be occupied tonight?" Laiten asked.

"No," Mothball replied, "but we didn't know that one would be either."

I dropped to all fours and assessed the coverage afforded by the opaque part of the window. "Stay low and stay close to the glass," I instructed Laiten. My knee complained as I used it to propel myself along the floor in what used to be an easier manoeuvre. I was holding Laiten back. We heard a chair scrape across the floor inside the room and I stopped. Laiten bumped into me.

"Keep going," he hissed. Laughter from inside the room gave me brief courage, and I crawled towards the end of the room where I found a matching alcove.

"We're clear," I announced in a whisper.

"Did you get a look inside?" Shifton asked.

"Didn't dare," Laiten replied.

"Just before the end of the corridor is another one on the left. Get down there and take that corridor." Shifton said.

I glanced around the corner at the room we had just crept by. The voices were at a steady volume and I hoped that meant they were still mid-discussion rather than about to leave. I turned to Laiten, "Ready?" I asked, he nodded.

I ran three steps and my knee seized, it stopped me dead. Laiten must have sensed me missing from his side. He came back and half dragged me to our next destination. Propping me up against the new corridor's wall, I was in too much pain to rejoice in its blue colouring. I sank to the floor.

"We can't stop, we need to get off this corridor, we're too close to that meeting. Where next, Shifton?" Laiten asked as I regained my breath.

"There's a huge storage area at the end of the corridor. I've only heard about it, I've never been in there. I did some digging, there's a rumour of another secret project being housed inside. If you can get in there, it may hold some answers. It's where the signal from the high-end tracker on Mickley's list is coming from."

"What do you mean, if?" I asked. I heard a sigh in my earpiece.

"It's the only door I cannot guarantee you'll open," she replied.

"Now you tell us!"

Mercifully the corridor was short. I hobbled beside Laiten towards the door. Once there, we exchanged a glance before I lined my face up at the scanner. I couldn't breathe. A red light appeared at the side of the door. I touched the panel. There were another two lights. I stared at the scanner again, and again, I held my breath. A second red light came on.

"Shif, we've only got one more go at this. If we fail, I'm expecting all hell to break loose."

"I'm working on a back route out. See that door on your left?" she asked, "if it opens, it leads to a quicker way out."

"Too many *ifs*" I said under my breath. "Ready?" I asked Laiten again.

"Do you want me to try?" he asked.

"Shif? What do you think?" I waited.

"It shouldn't trigger just for a change of retina, but it also won't reset the warning lights. Go for it."

Laiten took a deep breath and stared at the scanner. The

third light shone red for a fraction of a second before turning green. The door clicked open to reveal a brightly lit room.

"What the…?"

15
Fake Brews

After a brief, shocked pause at the door to the cavernous room, Laiten pushed me inside. Unseen from the office we stood by the door to let our brains process our surroundings. The room was a mixture of many projects. A robot construction area filled a far corner with inactive service bots at various stages of repair. No humans appeared to challenge our presence. The humans we found in the room had been encased in medical pods.

"The faces appear to match Mickley's list," Laiten announced. I joined him at the row of pods he was inspecting. "Here she is," he said.

"Tamara," I closed my eyes for a brief second before I checked the life signs on the panels of the pod. "She seems OK from what little I understand of these things," I said.

"They all do. Note no prosthetics are in the pods with them."

I looked down Tamara's tiny body through the small viewing window at face level and found Laiten was correct. "What the hell is going on?" I asked.

"Maybe they have to remove the limbs before going into the pods."

"OK, say that's true, why are they here in the first place?" Laiten shrugged at my question. "Are they all here?" I asked.

"No, I've doubled checked. Three people are missing. Is it any coincidence the missing ones were all dependent on round-the-clock care?"

"Are you getting all this Shif?" I'd almost forgotten she

could see what we saw and hear what we were saying.

"Yes, it's all being recorded for evidence."

Laiten finished transmitting the footage of each face along with their medical status to Shif and joined me at Tamara's pod.

"So, now what?" I began, "we've found most of them, they are alive, although whether their vitals are at optimum levels who can say?" I paused.

"They are," Mothball said in my head, surprising me again. "They are breathing unaided, they are being hydrated and receiving nutrition through the tubes."

"Half these people are missing legs." I threw my hands in the air, "we can't wake them up and get them all out, we need more help. Finding them was only ever half the job. What do we do next? Guys?" I asked when an answer was not forthcoming.

"Mickley's here," Shifton said.

I began to think I was a small cog in a much larger endeavour. "Mickley," I began, "I take it you've seen the feed? There are three missing."

"I can see. The missing three were terminally ill. Either they died of their illnesses or they were put down deliberately. They certainly were not well enough to leave the station on their own."

"What do you want us to do? There's a meeting going on up the corridor. There are only two of us and hardly any of these people will be able to walk if we can wake them. This is not a two-man job under these circumstances. Have you got a cavalry standing by that we don't know about?"

"Negative. Help is two days out from this point," Mickley said.

"In two days, there's no guarantee these people will still be here. I can't just leave them." The need to act began to overwhelm my common sense, and I took a breath. "If we take even one of them back," I reasoned, "the authorities, or whoever is responsible for this will notice. It's all or nothing, isn't it?"

"Yes," Mickley replied, "but at least we have proof and we know where they are. The problem is keeping the area secure until reinforcements arrive."

"I may have an idea," Mothball said.

"Any ideas at this point are welcome," I said.

"Cause an outbreak and quarantine the area," he said.

"Excuse me?" My voice hid more of my surprise and outrage than my face could.

"You want to let loose who knows what and risk the entire station? I cannot let you do that, Mothball."

"No, not a real outbreak," Mothball explained to the hard of understanding, "There are certain compounds which mimic deadly toxins and bacteria to the sensors. If we can trigger the sensors, we can lock the pods into that room," he said.

"That'll work for a while, but what happens when the sensors re-examine the area and see it's safe?" Laiten asked.

"You remember that time a quarantine locked down Ethan's 'Ol Bar?" Mothball asked.

I winced at the memory. "I couldn't get in for three days," I complained, "hang on, they fixed that glitch in the system and promised me it could never happen again." OK, I may have made a bit too much fuss over not being able to frequent my usual bar. So suspend me. No, wait... you can't...

"No, I fixed that glitch in that system," Shifton said, "I can easily un-fix it. I like it. We can trigger a spill alarm with something and I can break the system to lock down the room until the troops get here."

"Do the people in these pods need any further care?" I asked.

"No," Mothball's voice, "from what I can see all of them have everything they need to keep them comfortably unconscious until we can get them out.

"Have you hacked the pods yet?" I heard Shifton ask Mothball.

"Almost."

"What about just locking the room without triggering the sensors? Won't it look suspicious to trigger an outbreak? They'll be on heightened alert looking for a culprit." Laiten said.

"Doesn't matter either way. If I just lock it down," Shif began, "they'll suspect me because I fixed it in the first place."

"Pity Webster is so far away. We could have triggered something near him and let him take the blame," I muttered.

"Leave Webster out of it," Shifton said, "although…" there was a pause in communication which did not require the thump on the side of my head I inflicted on myself. Of her own accord, Shifton continued,

"Look around for any grey canisters labelled BTM-1115," Shifton instructed.

"Like we're just going to find exactly what we need in this room no-one has been in before," I muttered.

"It's a raw component used in the manufacture of the service bots in the corner."

"So how come they don't set the alarm off all the time?" I asked.

Laiten gave me a look somewhere between "What are you? An idiot?" and "Did you have to ask them that?"

"Its signature is unrecognisable when combined with Tea," Shifton said

"They do not make service bots out of tea," I said in disbelief.

"The letter T-3P7," Shifton's tone tried to convey patience, but I knew she was rolling her eyes at me.

"It's not here," I said running my eyes over fist-sized metal containers.

Distracted, Laiten walked to my location scrutinising a tiny cylinder he'd found. He looked at the canisters I'd been investigating and said, "Yeah, that's paint, Track."

"Of course it is," I muttered.

"I've found it," Laiten showed me his discovery. I took the canister and had to squint to make out the print on the side. He was correct, the tiny finger length canister was BTM-1115.

"OK, This thing must be the mini version. How many do we need?" I asked.

"Just the one," Shifton said.

"What will the sensors think it is?" I asked.

"Sepnid 7," Mothball began, "you know, the bastard that tried to kill me five times and took my legs in the process." It was the first time I'd heard bitterness about his situation in Mothball's voice. I couldn't sympathise enough, yet I had no clue what it must be like to be Mothball with no legs and the pallor of a corpse.

Distracted by my thoughts, I turned, jumped and swore loudly. I found myself up close and personal with a service bot which had come to life and begun its mission to rise up and take over the universe. "Shif… another Webster has woken up. What do we do?" I stared at the robot, "Artichoke, mandibles, beavers," I said in a panic, and no, I don't know where that last one came from either. The robot held its hand out to me. I took a step back.

"Track," Shifton said, "put the canister into the robot's hand."

"Why? Is he going to attack us if I don't?"

"Track, why the hell would you think it'll attack you? It's the same model as Ethan, and you talk to him every day," Shif said. I detected more eye rolling.

I spoke in my defence, "Ethan has skin and other human-like qualities. This one is all bare, menacing metal."

"You can't call what you taped to Ethan's head skin, it's half hanging off. Give," Shif said as the robot before me flexed the fingers of its outstretched hand twice.

Before I could stop myself from highlighting my slow reasoning skills, I blurted, "You're controlling this robot, aren't you, Shif?"

"Now he gets it," Mothball said.

I muttered something offensive under my breath and placed the canister in the robot's hand.

"Now what?" Laiten asked.

"You need to get out of that room before I crush the BTM-1115 or you won't be going anywhere for two days either," Shif said.

"I know I'm tired, Shif, but I'm not so dead upstairs that I don't realise if you can lock down this room, you can unlock it again. At any time," I added for emphasis.

"He's learning," Mothball said.

"So proud," I heard Shifton add. Laiten turned away too late to hide his grin.

"Are you coming?" I asked as I walked to the door.

"Pull the handle, Not the automatic switch. If anyone is out there, the switch will throw the door wide and you'll be seen," Shifton said.

"Gee, lessons in door procedures too. Aren't I a lucky and naïve boy?" I quipped, removing my hand from the switch as I wondered how the hell she knew I was about to make that mistake. It occurred to me later to remove the camera before I needed to use the toilet again. Oh shut up, I was tired. I pulled the door slightly ajar and stopped breathing. At the top of the corridor was a group of people I assumed were from the meeting. I felt my chest tighten as I looked at them, or rather one man in particular. I closed the door slightly so I couldn't be seen and squeezed my eyes tight shut. As each day went past I was more and more convinced I needed this break that wasn't a break. It tore my heart apart to tell myself the truth, but that guy out there that looked like my dead husband, couldn't possibly be him.

"Will it ever end?" I muttered under my breath as I opened the door and saw what could have been Jarner's twin walk away down the other corridor. It was heartbreaking.

"You OK?" Laiten asked at my hesitation.

"Yeah, just tired. Knee hurts. Nothing major," I lied, "Shif, what's our exit strategy?"

"That door outside the room, I think I've broken into it, but I won't know for sure until you try to open it."

"And how soon after Webster 2 here crushes the BTMwhatever does all hell break loose?" I asked.

"Ten seconds at most," she replied, "but don't worry, I'll wait until you're clear. You won't want to be near it, anyway."

"I thought you said it was safe?" I failed to keep the alarm out of my voice.

"It is safe," she said, "it stinks so much, people throw up when they smell it."

"And there are no cameras down here, right?" I asked wondering if there was a way to prove to my damaged mind the man at the bottom of the corridor wasn't Jarner.

"No, not in that section, they re-installed them all in the public areas rather than buy new ones," she replied.

I checked the corridor again. "Clear?" I asked Laiten to verify what I was seeing.

"Clear," he said, frowning at my request.

I opened the door wide and headed towards our escape route. Laiten closed the door to the medical pods with a click. I glanced behind me to check he was close and noticed the number on the door we had just left. Eight, seven, four, six. I had been so desperate to get inside I hadn't noticed it before. Searching my pockets I retrieved the scrap of paper Tamara's dad had left on the table as they left Carrie's. Same number. Just how far did this thing reach?

"You going to open the door?" Laiten asked.

I looked at the screen and moved away. "You do it, my eyes are broken," I said. Laiten probably thought I meant they wouldn't unlock doors. He had no reason to suspect I was questioning my sanity and seeing my dead husband in other people's faces. I was shaken and stood behind Laiten while he lined up, had his eyes scanned and pushed the unlocked door open a fraction.

"Where the hell is this?" he asked.

I peered over his shoulder and pushed him through the doorway. The area in front of us was dimly lit, and I recognised it immediately. Closing the one-way door behind me I muttered,

"How the hell we ended up here, I'll never know."

"Huh?" Laiten still didn't recognise his surroundings.

"Come on, I need a drink," I hobbled past him, through the storage area and emerged near the robot charging station.

"Hello Track, would you like a rum mix?" Ethan asked.

16
How did we end up here?

"Make it a large one please, Ethan," I replied.

"I'll have what he's having," Laiten said turning his back on the robot and leaning his elbows on the bar behind him. "Not many people in here tonight," he said as the only other patron left. "Make that no people in here tonight. Something I said? Do we smell?"

"It's late," I muttered. We were an around the clock station, but those not covering a shift pattern still slept during the station's chosen nighttime hours.

I pulled myself onto a stool as Ethan set down two drinks in front of us. We both muttered a thank you. "I'll get these," I said as I scanned my thumb.

"You are very welcome, gentlemen," Ethan replied. The robot glitched for a second as the alarm we had been expecting sounded three times to alert the Authority personnel to check in. The alarm stopped at three to alert the rest of the station that whatever had occurred was not a public risk.

"Doesn't stop people from panicking, though, does it?" I thought out loud, "I mean if the general population had a clue where the alarm originated they," I downed my drink, "they'd see it was nowhere near them and carry on."

"Putting the location up of an alarm will only highlight those areas which are secret and cause all kinds of speculation," Laiten murmured. He was right.

I pushed my glass towards Ethan and didn't have to say anything before he nodded and made me another drink.

"You'd better get going," I said. Laiten gave me a blank look. "The alarm, I know we know why it sounded. We don't need the Authority to suspect we know why. You need to check in at least to offer your assistance."

"For a minute," Laiten paused to finish his drink, "I thought you were going to embark on one of those *they know, we know, they know, he knows* monologues."

"Way too tired," I replied.

"OK, I'll check in. I expect Lena will send me around with breakfast in the morning. We seem to have started a habit, better keep it up."

I muttered something in agreement as Laiten left the bar. My eyes drooped.

"Shif, Mothball, are you still here?" I asked of my inner voices.

"Yes."

"Still here."

"Me too," Mickley announced.

I'd forgotten about Mickley. "Sorry Mickley, so she jabbed one of these things in your neck too?" I asked.

"I already had one," Mickley replied.

"We shouldn't be in contact for a while until we know how much impact we've made."

"Agreed."

"I'll finish my drink and see if I can make it back to my apartment without being kidnapped, beaten up, shot at or decontaminated." I tapped the side of my neck and just to make sure I was alone in my own head, I said, "Can you hear me?" There was no answer. I drank the rest of my second drink, which had gone straight to my head and got up to leave. "Thanks, Ethan, see you." I staggered to the door.

"I'll see you on Nartern Eleven," Ethan said. I stopped and turned, jarring my knee and asked,

"What did you say?"

"I said, Goodbye Track, see you later."

"Of course you did," I slurred.

I meandered my way back to my apartment. Even though

I took the shortcuts avoiding all the busy public areas, it still took as long to get home. My knee twinged at regular intervals and I found myself leaning on several walls. My eyes were dry and tired. Pity no-one saw me, the entertainment value of the faces I pulled trying to focus on my surroundings was priceless. I walked past my door before I realised I was home. Turning around, I stomped my way back as if I was a robot underwater.

My eyeballs almost fell out of their sockets as I stretched my face to scan into my apartment. I was aware my expression also allowed for my tonsils to be scanned. Pity that's not a thing.

As my door mocked me for a third time refusing to open, I threw everything at it. ID card, handprint, eyeballs, tonsils. Finally, the bloody thing relented. I forgot I was leaning on the door when it opened and staggered into my apartment like a reluctant performer being pushed centre stage. I resisted the urge to grin at a fake audience and do a few high kicks. It didn't take much resistance.

Banyon's ears wiggled, and he tilted his head at me. "What's that? The factory setting of how to react to your owner when he walks into the room making an arse of himself?" I asked. I wasn't surprised when he didn't answer.

Turning around and causing a dizzy spell, I staggered, groaning towards my front door to shut out the world. They only reason I didn't allow my knees to buckle and deposit me onto the floor is that it's bloody uncomfortable.

I stared at my comfortable chair, lined my body up and gave one concerted effort to launch myself at it. Something in the middle of the floor tripped me and I stumbled forwards, landing untidily in my chair. I seem to recall saying, "Ta daaaa" before I fell asleep or passed out, you choose.

***

I awoke with a start. Listening for a few seconds, I expected to hear Laiten hammering on my door again. I made a note to put in a complaint that my baked goods had yet to arrive when I realised it wasn't him. There was no noise from Banyon either. With no idea what had woken me, I had a quick look around the apartment, saw no intruders, ninjas or robots taking over the station, and decided to have a shower. I moaned loudly as the hot water hit my muscles. After a few seconds of audible appreciation, I heard Banyon join my chorus with a death-growl of his own.

"I really must get you fixed," I said, as Banyon's cute little face snarled at me. Having again ascertained a lack of people wanting to attack me in my apartment, I wandered into the bedroom to get dressed.

I heard my front door open as I was pushing my feet into my boots. Reaching for my weapon, I crept towards my bedroom door as Banyon scampered over to the ninja-robot-uprising assailant. I swung myself around the doorway with my weapon pointing ahead. I quickly raised it towards the ceiling.

"Sorry, I should have knocked," Laiten said.

"You think? You're late," I stated.

"We didn't set a time," he replied.

I grunted and looked at the bag Laiten was carrying, no doubt containing the baked goods I was expecting a full ten minutes ago. Laiten handed over the bag as I attached my weapon to my belt.

"I'll make coffee," he said, "how's your knee?"

"Snhufa," I sprayed crumbs across the room. Given a second to chew and swallow I said, "Not too bad thanks. I trust you're OK," I asked assessing his impossibly young face as he brought coffee to the table. He nodded. "How was the alarm we triggered received last night?" I asked.

"With exactly the amount of disinterest you'd expect," he replied.

From my chair, I could see my front door. After frowning at Laiten for a few seconds, I asked, "Was my door open when you arrived?"

"No, sorry, I stopped in on Shifton and Mothball last night after the alarm and happened to mention bringing you breakfast and you apparently going on a short course of death when you sleep. She gave me access. I can cancel it," he said.

I shook my head. With the amount of action I'd seen recently, I could use a guy with the ability to fight off someone with their hands around my throat. "You can probably study that at the COC," I quipped.

"Huh?"

"Short course of death. Two-day or three-day course, do you think?" I asked.

Laiten smirked, "Family saying, you could set off a nuke near some of my relatives when they're sleeping and they'd never notice."

"That's because they'd be dead from the nuke."

"OK, bad example. You know what I mean."

We sat in amiable silence for a while drinking and eating whatever it was Laiten had brought. I couldn't quite place it, but I was hungry and not taking my time to taste. "Do you think you can interrogate the system to find information on Hegland and what he was working on before he arrived back on the station?" I asked brushing crumbs from my clothes and refraining from calling Banyon over to pretend to eat them. "From where I'm sitting," I continued, "it looks like he moved to the wrong side. He wouldn't have attacked Shifton if he hadn't."

"And we know for sure it's Hegland in that box?" Laiten asked.

"Shifton knows what she's doing," I replied, "she'll have checked DNA, fingerprints, teeth, serial numbers on anything inside him holding serial numbers. Unless someone faked up teeth and fingerprints and gave him a massive dose of Hegland's blood, it's Hegland." I wasn't sure how I felt. Disappointed in him, sad at losing him, doubtful he was acting against us. All of those emotions. I needed answers.

"I can try. He may be off the grid and classified though. I may not find anything," he replied.

"See if you can talk to Wicklow. Before he went under, I saw Hegland having an animated conversation with her at

Carrie's. I'd love to know if that conversation is relevant."

"I'll try, but I'm the new boy. Not everyone has warmed to me yet. Especially not enough to tell me anything meaningful," he said.

"Just flash that impossibly young smile. Or," I said with animation, "do one of those little boy lost looks at Wicklow, you might have more chance with her."

"I'm not sure which one of us you've insulted the most," Laiten said, balling up the empty bag and throwing it in my direction.

"Now you've done it," I said as Banyon leapt into action and chased the ball down. "He's set for a repeat of five, then you're off the hook," I stated, watching Laiten throw and Banyon fetch.

Amuse-the-human time complete, Banyon returned to his bed. "Whatever you do," I said, "don't let on Hegland is dead."

Laiten stared at me for a few seconds before saying, "You remember this face is from a much younger person, right? I have investigated things before."

"Sorry, I blame my situation. I haven't been at a loose end for years. My brain is turning to mush."

"You've got a long time to go yet," he said.

"Don't remind me," I muttered.

"So what are your plans for today?" he asked.

"Were you sent as an entertainment coordinator to make sure I don't disintegrate during the next three months?"

"Something like that," Laiten grinned.

"I'm deeply hurt. I thought you were only here for my scintillating conversation."

"So?" he asked.

"Shi… you actually want an answer? No bloody idea. Maybe I'll go down to the COC and see if they have anything other than knitting or sewing courses."

"Very practical skill, sewing," he said.

I gave him my "this conversation has ended but I'm too lazy to turn my back on you" stare. I didn't do it very well because he continued,

"Maybe there's a mechanics course," he said with hope.

"There isn't, I checked. OK, I'll go down there and see if there's anything I can do that won't make me feel like shooting it after five minutes."

"Got to get to work," Laiten said walking his coffee mug and bag to the kitchen, "I'll let you wash up, it'll fill thirty seconds of your day."

"I can't wait," I muttered before remembering my manners and yelling "thank you for breakfast" at my closed front door.

I picked up the jacket I had only removed before my shower and frowned at its weight. Remembering the mysterious container Shifton had me retrieve from Research last night, I searched the pockets and placed the item on my desk. I stared at it expecting it to explode or stink. It did neither. I threw a goodbye over my shoulder to Banyon, slung my jacket over my arm and left for the dreaded COC.

There was a brief lull in conversation when I entered the area. Almost the whole room resumed their dialogues at a louder volume as if to make up for noticing me.

My gaze was drawn to Jarner's artwork on the wall.

No. I turned around and left. The memories were too raw.

17
Eight Seven Four Six

"Track," I heard in my head and stumbled a couple of steps towards a wall just outside the COC. I grinned at a group of people who gave me a wide berth. I spent a few seconds contemplating a trip to medical to report voices in my head. My thoughts were interrupted by, "Track," I looked behind me. Apart from the retreating group, there was no-one around to sound close enough to call my name. "Track, press your damned neck," I raised my head slowly as realisation dawned and pressed my damned neck.

"Shifton?" I said under my breath.

"Finally," she said.

"I thought we'd agreed not to contact each other," I complained.

"We did, but this is serious."

I waited. "Well?" I muttered trying not to move my lips in case someone saw me talking to myself.

"Tamara's pod has malfunctioned."

I almost tripped over my feet at the news. Before I could question Shifton, she continued,

"She's alive, but she's only got a few hours to live. As far as we can tell, no-one else is bothering to monitor any of the pods."

I breathed through my fury at the blatant disregard for human welfare. When I had regained enough composure to mutter without annihilating my knuckles on the surrounding walls, I asked, "Am I on my own this time?"

"Yeah, sorry, Laiten can't get away without looking

suspicious. You need to break her out. She will run out of oxygen. Those pods are akin to coffins when they lose power and they're nowhere near any external backup supplies."

"If the power has already gone, how do I get her out of stasis?" I asked as I took a turn into a deserted outlet selling old gaming tech other stations had long since abandoned.

"That's the thing," Shif continued, "the pod has an internal power supply, when it fails, it has a short-term backup power supply. It's enough to sustain life while the person is brought out of stasis before all power is lost.

I stopped in my tracks. "Are you telling me these pods bring people around, just so they know they're about to suffocate?"

"Yes."

"That's barbaric," I kept my voice under control as two people entered the domain of depressing tech.

"I know," Shif continued, "the pods are obsolete. We've found the schematics on the system. They were designed to open on power failure, but that mechanism never worked. The entire shipment was supposed to be recycled. Why we have some here, we can only speculate."

I had heard enough. I still had cards and ID on me. Of course, it was the middle of the day, Research was going to be packed with people… researching, I was bound to be discovered. I had to try, I couldn't leave the little girl to that fate.

"I'm heading down to the lifts," I said under my breath. One of the youths who must have had younger hearing than me gave me a look and moved further away from the old man muttering to himself.

"No, wait," Shif said in my head.

Before answering her, I left the outlet and muttered, "Waiting,"

"Go to Ethan's," Shifton instructed.

I was in the middle of a group of people drifting at the universe's slowest pace towards the lifts. They weren't talking loud enough to mask the sound of me muttering like a madman. I wasn't comfortable talking out-loud on this implanted tech no-one could see. An idea I kicked myself for not thinking of earlier occurred and I grabbed my comms unit from my belt. Hoping no-one contacted me on it, I pretended I was using it.

"Why do I need to go there?" I asked in a near normal voice, "I thought that door only opened from the other side.

"Working on it."

It was bad enough I had one voice in my head, my simple brain couldn't cope with the sudden change in voice to Mothball. I relaxed my wide eyes and got over the feeling I'd just been inappropriately groped.

In a nearby lift, I lowered my face away from camera coverage and asked, "Am I still registering as Hegland or doesn't it matter anymore?"

"Shit," I heard Shifton's voice.

"I take it that's a no."

"I changed you back last night. Hang on."

By the time the lift had reached the floor I required, I exited a new man. Or, at least a newly dead one. On autopilot, I walked to the bar.

"Hello Track, are you just off night shift?" Ethan asked. Apparently, Shifton's incognito powers only went so far. Ethan's face was beyond repair. A flap of purple synthetic skin hung off the side of his metal cheek.

"Can I just?" I began, "You've got something just…" I reached over the bar and pulled on the offending flap of skin and the remainder dropped onto the counter. I swear Ethan's immobile features looked sad at the loss of his face.

"Track," Mothball's voice made me jump, "try the door."

I walked around the bar and past the charging station through to Ethan's storage area. Unless you knew it was there, the imperceptible crack between the door and the wall was easily missed.

The door clicked open, and I slid through the gap to be met by Webster. Whatever I was expecting on the other side of the door, it wasn't the communicatively challenged Webster.

"Er, raspberries, mastication, fireflies…" I hissed as Webster completed the retreat he had already started.

"It's OK," Shifton's voice jolted in my ears, "I've overridden his programming."

I was too preoccupied to ask why she hadn't done so last night. I found myself at the door to the vast storage room having my eyes scanned before I remembered it might not work. In the distance behind me, I could hear voices moving closer. The door popped open. I was not used to being this lucky. I slid into the room and breathed in the stench of a million corpses, rotting vegetation, bad eggs, feet, sweaty armpits and… thyme.

"Holy Uncle of Victon." I spluttered, completely forgetting about the stench associated with the substance we released the night before. "I'm going to die, aren't I?" I said as I tried not to breathe, yet still remain alive.

"No," Shifton said, "I told you, it's perfectly safe."

I coughed, choked and swallowed the gross taste of the air I would never get out of anything attached to my person. Tears streamed down my cheeks as I said, "I don't believe you." After a few seconds to regain my composure, I managed, "Why are there no guards? Why is no-one trying to find out what happened in here last night?" I asked.

"I don't think the lives of the people in that room are important enough to distract the Authority from their delegates."

I took a deep breath from my armpit, but it was useless, nothing detracted from the toxic stench. Coughing, I made my way to Tamara's pod. "Oh fuck, tell me what to do to get her out of there. She's awake, and she's panicking," I said as I tried to catch the little girl's attention through the clear window at her head. Her open eyes were beyond seeing reason.

"Three latches underneath, pull them," Shifton said, urgency present in her voice.

I pulled the latches, and the lid popped up a hand's width.

"It's OK, I'm going to get you out, Tamara, keep still." My words went unheeded as the little girl thrashed in blind panic whilst I raised the lid of her potential coffin. I leant over her to pick her up, but a tiny fist connected with my nose. How a child her size could pack such a punch was beyond me. I recoiled, my hand instinctively moving to my nose. I expected to feel shattered bones or at least bring my hand away covered in blood. There was nothing. Yet, still, I was assaulted by the smell of the universe's biggest turd. I approached the little girl with the thrashing arms with caution.

No longer entombed, Tamara had calmed. Tears of panic were still running down the side of her head towards her ears as she hiccupped the words, "You smell nice."

I took a few seconds to accept anyone would consider this room smelt anything other than apocalyptic. "I'm going to pick you up, OK?" I said. Tamara nodded. "I need you to keep your eyes closed and don't make a sound. Can you do that?" I asked. I didn't want her to see the other pods, she didn't need that vision in her life. She nodded again.

As I picked her up and held her vertically to my chest I was shocked at how light she was without legs. She buried her head in my shoulder.

Forgetting where I was I drew in a regrettable deep breath. "I've got her," I said to Shifton and Mothball, "I don't suppose there's any way you know if anyone is in the corridor outside?" I asked.

"No, sorry, you will have to look. The door is still unlocked," Shifton said.

"Stay very still and quiet," I whispered to Tamara. She nodded her head against my shoulder. Before looking, I closed my eyes and begged for a clean getaway. When I opened them and peered around the door, I saw the back of one retreating figure at the other end of the corridor.

"Still and silent," I said again and left room eight seven

four six, closing the door with a click behind me.

I made a dash for the door leading to Ethan's storage area. The day wouldn't have been the same if I hadn't twisted my knee on the way. Gasping cleaner air, the smell still lingered in my nostrils. I muttered a few vegetables and a rodent at Webster for good measure as I rushed past and manhandled myself and my innocent, quietly sobbing cargo into the relative safety of Ethan's back office. "OK, we're in Ethan's," I said. Clinging to Tamara with one arm, I wiped the tears away from my face with the other. "I never want to experience that stench again," I said.

"You did well not to throw up," Shifton replied.

"Trust me, I was tempted. I'm going to reek of this stuff forever."

"No, you'll be fine, I've got something here that will stop the smell," she said.

"What are you going to do? Cut off my nose?" I thought I heard Shifton say the word "idiot", but I was probably mistaken.

"Now that you've breathed it in, don't eat or drink anything until you clean it off, it'll ruin how things taste."

"Pity," I muttered thinking about the copious amounts of alcohol a few feet away.

"Bring Tamara to us. It's the safest place for her."

"What if there's another incident like the other night? Are you sure?" I asked, referencing the demise of my former partner.

"I'm sure, she'll be safe here. But Track, she can't be seen. If the wrong person recognises her, the whole thing is ruined and everyone involved will be at risk."

"OK," I said looking around me for something to use for an awful idea I had. "Is the room secure again?" I asked, "Is the quarantine still in place?"

"Yes," Mothball said. I was too preoccupied with my search to be surprised by his voice. I moved Tamara awkwardly in my arms, I had little experience with children.

"Is there any chatter about that room on the system?" I

asked.

"No," I heard Mothball sigh, "it's as if nothing has happened."

I bit down my anger as I found what I was looking for. How one man could possess so much luggage I don't know. The last time I'd brought a major amount of spares to fix Ethan, I'd done so in a wheeled case. His gratitude had left me paralytic, and I'd stashed the case out back and forgotten to pick it up.

I had a dreadful suspicion my next step was not going to be easy. "Tamara, honey, I need to get you to safety. And the best way to do that is for you to be inside this case. Can you do that for me?" I asked. She looked up at me with wide eyes full of fear and looked down at the case I was dragging with my free hand. The little girl reacted in the only way I thought possible for someone young or old who had just woken up in a sealed metal box. She panicked and screamed.

I will never forgive myself for the chokehold I put her in. For the life of me, I had no idea how else I would get her undetected through Si-Cross Four's busy corridors unless she was unconscious. I felt unworthy of even the fetid air in room eight seven four six.

18
The Body in the Case

Tamara's body fell limp in my arms. My level of self-loathing couldn't reach any higher. There was a distance to travel with the unpredictability of someone who could regain consciousness at any moment. I already knew I wouldn't be able to incapacitate Tamara a second time. I just didn't have that in me. I laid her on the floor and opened the case. Shaking my head, I discovered it was full of things about which I'd have time to say, "so that's where that went," later. Time was against me.

Checking the now empty case for sharp edges, I bundled Tamara's limp body inside and closed the clasps. I turned to be met by Ethan. "Hi Ethan, bye Ethan," I muttered and dragged the case behind me as I limped out of Ethan's 'Ol Bar.

Our trip would be fine all the time Tamara was unconscious. People were used to me dragging a case of spares around the station. This was no different, I tried to tell myself. If she awoke before we reached Shifton's room, I would be arrested as soon as she began thrashing around, and rightly so.

As I dragged the case behind me through the station's corridors, I knew getting to my destination undiscovered was a huge ask. Odds were I would get so far and Tamara would scream the place down. In my mind, as I continued on my journey, I played "guess the arresting detective." My money was on Wicklow. There were options of the long route with fewer people, or the short route with more people. I chose the latter. I made it to the last lift which would take me to Shifton's floor. Holding my breath, I entered the empty lift and breathed a sigh of relief until a hand forced its way through the gap of the closing doors. I was face to face with Beynard.

As the doors closed, he stared at the floor numbers whilst I avoided any risk of seeing a Nartern Eleven message and looked anywhere else. We began our high-speed trip in silence, for which I was grateful. I thought I was getting away with it until Beynard spoke, "Keeping busy?" he eyed my case.

"Trying to," I hoped my nonchalant tone masked the dance my internal organs were performing.

"Anything at the COC of any interest?" he asked.

I shrugged, "Not much."

"I'm sure you'll find something to occupy your time," Beynard said.

Tamara sneezed. I resisted the urge to close my eyes in defeat and instead stared directly ahead. I was about to be locked up for child abduction and share my personal space with a selection of Si-Cross Four's petty thieves and anarchists. I briefly wondered how Byrod's jaw was healing and mused I would soon have the opportunity to find out first hand.

Tamara sneezed again, louder than before. I caught sight of Beynard looking down at my case. This was it. I was about to be cuffed and led unceremoniously through the throng of my former colleagues, enduring looks of shame and disgust on their faces.

The lift doors opened onto Authority Four's lobby area. I took a step forward to follow Beynard as he left the lift and I stopped dead when he called out, "Enjoy the rest of your day Track."

The doors closed. Beynard was gone, and I was left with a void in my head where all my coherent thoughts used to reside.

"Almost there kiddo," I muttered more for my benefit

than Tamara's. A wave of fatigue took me by surprise. The lack of adrenaline shocked me. Beynard's failure to react to the little girl's sneeze astonished me. I almost missed my floor. As the doors of the lift were closing on Shifton's floor, I stepped out into the quiet corridor. "Yeah, yeah," I grumbled to my knee as it made its presence known. By the time I had reached Shifton's room, I was ready for painkillers and some recalibration of whatever she had implanted into my knee. And a holiday somewhere in the middle of a riot would be less disturbing too.

My dry eyes widened in my attempt to gain access via the scanner. "It's Track," I called as I entered the room. My shoulders dropped, and I realised I'd been carrying a planet's worth of tension in my body. So much for nonchalantly wandering the corridors of the station with a case full of innocent spares. The door closed and hid me from the outside world.

Reaching out to unfasten the clasps of the case, I made sure Tamara wouldn't fall when I lifted the lid. I tried to keep a distance between me and her flailing arms. Yes, that's me, Detective Track, terrified of the wrath of a tiny disabled child.

Large dark eyes stared up at me from the case. Two arms reached for me. I bend down to pick Tamara up, she would have been well within her rights to jab her fingers into my eyes, but instead, she threw her arms around my neck and buried her head into my shoulder.

"I am so sorry I had to do that to you," I whispered in her ear. I was both horrified at my actions and relieved she appeared to come through the ordeal physically unharmed. Only time would tell what her mental state would make of it.

"Can I go home now?" she asked.

My heart sank further. Shifton approached from across the room. I took a step backwards, not because I didn't trust Shifton's lethality around children, Shif wasn't dangerous in that way, but Tamara had been through enough and sometimes Shif looked bloody scary.

"Hey Tamara," Shifton called.

I braced myself for the incoming kicks from Tamara's stumps, or maybe a bite on my shoulder followed by an ear-splitting scream.

Tamara turned to the voice and let out a shriek, "Shifton!" she screamed and launched herself out of my arms into Shifton's.

So everybody knew everybody else on this station and no-one had seen fit to tell me. Whatever, I was knackered. I collapsed into the nearest chair and rubbed at my knee having passed Tamara over.

Mothball walked around the desk towards me and indicated my knee.

"You want me to take a look at that?" he asked.

"Please," I pulled up my trouser leg and struggled to expose my knee beneath the fabric. Mothball whistled.

"That's swollen. Hang on," he hobbled away.

"No wonder the bloody thing hurts," I muttered to myself. My knee was doing an excellent impression of a gnarly stalla fruit, larger than the average fist but purple and knobbly like it had knuckles all over it. Mothball returned with what looked like nuclear waste enclosed in a clear rubber bag. The luminescent green gel glowed as he laid it on my knee.

"Cold pack," he announced as he reached over for another chair to raise my leg. I thanked him and allowed myself a few seconds to close my eyes. Across the room, I could hear Shifton explaining to Tamara why she couldn't go home yet, but that she would be able to do so soon. I didn't hear any screaming, so I took this to be a good sign.

I must have dozed off for a few minutes. When I awoke I saw Tamara asleep in Capybara Corner. The remains of a snack and drink sat on an upturned box at the edge of the den.

"How is she?" I asked Shifton.

"She's fine, tired. It seems strange, but everyone is exhausted when they wake up from stasis. You'd think the enforced sleep would be beneficial, it's very draining," she said. I nodded. I hadn't experienced it myself, but I'd heard stories of people taking days to recover after a stint asleep in a bio-pod.

"I know you don't get much foot-traffic here, but Tamara can't stay here indefinitely. How long until backup arrives on the station?" I asked and squirmed as I tried for a more comfortable position on my chairs. I heard Mothball hit keys and mutter to himself before announcing,

"At least twelve hours. Even when they get here, there's added security due to another group of visiting dignitaries."

I groaned, "It's the season for it, apparently."

"There are always visiting dignitaries. We're just rarely hiding bodies and small children when they arrive," Shifton slumped in a chair and wiped her hands over her eyes.

"And what's the plan when backup does arrive?" I asked.

Shifton shook her head. "I don't know. They're keeping that to themselves, probably for security reasons."

"Whoever they are, happen to be running this thing. Out of the loop again," I muttered.

Shifton ignored my complaint, "I had thought about telling Tamara's parents she was here and trying to get them off the station. I'm not convinced we could get them out undetected with all the additional security."

I shook my head.

"And if we handed her back to her parents, at this stage, I'm not convinced they would stay out of sight of whoever took her in the first place," Mothball added.

"So Tamara stays here," Shifton said.

"For now, at least. I should get back. I'm not sure what the Authority is expecting me to fill my three months with, but I think I'd feel more secure window shopping the outlets than hiding away in places they don't associate me with. Are you OK to look after her for now?" Before I'd finished the sentence, Shifton nodded.

Having checked Tamara was still sleeping peacefully and given my nuclear cold pack to Mothball, I left with my promised anti-stink device. My gut told me to go back to Ethan's and have a drink. After all, that's where people could almost always find me. However, the newly found door to research put me off. For all I knew somebody in Research Division may have looked through the plans and decided to open up that wall into the back of the bar just for quick access to alcohol at the end of the day. It's something I'd have considered. In all my time sitting at that bar I had never seen anyone come out of the back. Maybe the turnover in personnel was so high no-one considered venturing into anything other than their assigned rooms. It was a blank door, it could have been a cleaning cupboard.

How long I'd been limping along was anyone's guess. I found myself at the exclusive end of the outlets staring blindly at items for sale only wealthy visitors could afford. The station was awash with people selling high-end merchandise they could ill-afford themselves. The unfairness did not escape me. Several investigations had been made into thefts of items sold on the underground to fund some unfortunate's medical bills, or feed a family with something other than tasteless stodge.

There was no job satisfaction in arresting someone for theft who only had the welfare of their family in mind. But the law was the law. Even if the wealthy wouldn't miss one high-end piece of glassware which could feed a worker's family for months, we still had to carry out the arrests. It gave me no joy to see a family disintegrate over the removal of their main food earner for weeks as they served out their sentence working disgusting jobs for barely enough food to feed themselves. Their families rationed what they had or relied on the goodwill of people like Carrie or those who also barely had enough until their main earner returned and the cycle began again.

I'd heard my name called three times before my brain convinced me to respond. Turning, I saw a junior detective. Unlike some who worked up the ranks, this one had none of the timidity of his fellow pay-grade. He was a cocky little bastard, who registered on the Track-O-meter as someone to avoid rather than learn his name. I thought of Laiten and how I misjudged him before I knew he was a thirty-something behind the transplanted face of an early twenty-something.

"Detective Track, you need to come with me. Beynard wants you."

I think I understood it then, Beynard knew I wouldn't hurt a child and rather than put her through further trauma he let me take her to safety before having me arrested. I frowned and shook my head at my unlikely scenario. The junior detective assumed I was resisting and drew his weapon.

19

Bring the Bonus Underpants

The walk to Authority Four was the longest I had ever taken. I couldn't blame that on my knee, it was the overriding sense of dread which filled me.

After the junior detective had held his weapon on me, I threw my hands in the air and insisted I wasn't resisting. I was grateful he lowered his gun and allowed me to walk unrestrained into my former place of work. The more time elapsed, the less likely it felt I would ever go back in a professional capacity. A few people smiled, waved and acknowledged my existence as I walked through the dilapidated furniture I missed so much. It had been a couple of days and their attitude towards me had changed. Gone was the "ignore on pain of death" atmosphere. I had become someone with nothing else in their life but work. Not true, I reminded myself. I had Banyon, a few friends and people I tried to help with my in-expertise for mechanics.

I waved to Wicklow. She smiled at me and frowned at my nameless companion. I turned to see the man had reached for his weapon as I waved. I was unaware of any secret powers I may have in my hands, but in case my escort knew something I didn't, I kept my hands by my side. I didn't want to unleash a fireball at anyone, or maybe a tsunami, possibly a swarm of flying miniature capybara…

"Thank you…" Beynard muttered as we entered his lair. There was a mumbled word which followed. I assumed it was the detective's name. Beynard's poor enunciation meant it remained a mystery. "Track, sit."

I wasn't in the mood to bark. I sat and awaited my fate.

"I have possible bad news," Beynard began.

An arrest rarely started like that. I felt my face screw up in confusion and waited for my commanding officer to continue.

"I have received reports from the department Hegland was working for that he has missed several check-ins."

Somewhere in an alternate reality, a version of me completely lost control at that moment sagged in the chair with his head in his hands, blew out a breath of relief and a loud "whoop". In my reality, I held it together. "He's probably deep undercover. I'm sure he's missed check-ins before. I know I did."

"Yes, you hold the record for missed check-ins," Beynard stated without amusement. "What the department is unclear about is why Hegland has appeared on this station's location logs a few times. We are trying to track him now."

"He's not showing up on any location monitors at the moment?" I asked and immediately pleaded with the universe for Beynard not to check. He tapped buttons on his desk. I could see a blue glow of results reflecting on his clothing. Refusing to blink, I hoped Shifton had remembered to switch me back again. The last thing I needed was for Beynard to see Hegland's ID sitting where I was.

"No. Hegland is not currently on the station. When was the last time you heard from him?"

The full realisation that this interview was about my partner's whereabouts and not my abduction of an unconscious little girl hit me and I stifled a sigh of relief before answering. "Weeks ago. Before he went under. I was given to believe this job was deep with a no communication clause."

"It was. That doesn't mean he didn't reach out to anyone. I believe you also hold the record for breaking that rule."

"I always got results," I said in my defence.

Beynard's acknowledgement was a frown and a reluctant, "Hmmm. If you hear from him I expect you to let me know.

I know you won't, but it would be remiss of me not to remind you of Authority protocol."

I nodded, and we sat in awkward silence for a few seconds.

"How are you finding the COC?" he asked.

I almost asked him what his fascination was with the COC, but refrained. "It's not really my thing. Although I noticed a pole dancing course that might be amusing to infiltrate."

Beynard's eyes narrowed and his lips resembled the thin line of his lazy written signature. I felt I was missing something. To ease the awkward lull in conversation, I said, "If there was a mechanics course or engineering…" I paused, "something to give me an idea of how to fix artificial limbs properly with some lasting effect, that would be of huge interest."

"Not going to happen. As far as the Authority is concerned, they don't exist, you know that."

Beynard saw the shade of crimson my face had turned and held up his hands. "I don't agree with it either. You're not the only one who thinks the whole situation was mishandled from the beginning of the outbreak. They haven't even told us what caused it. You know what I know. Somehow, Sepnid 7 got out. We don't know where from or how. It is blatantly clear that we have to look after our own because no-one will step in and do it for us."

I wondered if the sentiment stretched to him looking after my career. I held my tongue, the callous comparison of my job against the health and wellbeing of a discarded section of society was unworthy of even my foulest mood.

In other stories, I'm sure the detective would stand up from the chair at this point and announce they were leaving in a surly tone. I was comfortable and enjoyed being around *my people*. Even if Beynard's office always filled me with a vision of being ripped a new one.

I stared at Beynard or rather through him, zoning out for a while. He said something I didn't catch, and I blinked and shook my head, "Eh?"

"I said, tell me if Hegland gets in touch."

I nodded. "Will do," I was glued to the chair.

Beynard's look screamed "what are you waiting for?" before relenting and spelling it out for me. "You may leave."

My face fell comically and I muttered, "If I have to." I groaned as I dragged myself out of the chair and staggered to the door.

"Oh and Track,"

I turned, "Why do people do that?" I asked.

"What?"

"I was sitting there for ages and you said nothing, now I'm almost through the door you've got something to say. Why do people do that?"

"I don't know, sign up for the psychology course at the COC and ask them."

"Well?" I asked.

"Oh, yes, check lost property on your way out, there might be spares you can use."

"Thanks," I muttered. I wasn't surprised he knew about my fixing days, I was surprised he openly didn't disapprove in some way. Maybe I had him all wrong.

***

Several hours after I had stashed my spare "ooh look, it's one of these", "oh great it's a widget" and "I don't know what this is but I'm sure it will be useful," I found myself walking through the deserted corridors I had purposely chosen to look for human interaction. What can I say? I craved human contact, but I'd rather do it without the humans. Yeah, I know it doesn't make sense, so, sue me. I tapped my neck. "Track calling Shifton. This is Track calling Shifton. Are you there Shifton?" I muttered under my breath.

"I thought we weren't going to contact each other," she said.

"Change of plans. I'm bored," I could see her rolling her eyes at the man-child's inability to find anything on the vast space station with which to amuse himself.

"You'd better come in anyway, I have news."

I smiled an inane grin. My day had improved, assuming the news wasn't another death, or outbreak or kidnap. My face fell, and I turned awkwardly towards the lift. "On my way."

***

"Whoa, you kids aren't fucking about, are you?" The impressive array of weaponry on the bench was being checked, prepped and loaded by the alarming combination of Mothball, Shifton and Tamara. "Should she be doing that?" my eyes were so wide they risked falling from their sockets.

"Relax," Mothball said, "she's only checking the charge on the energy cells."

"What does fucking mean?" The small child asked. Shifton gave me an expectant look.

"It's a naughty word I shouldn't have used in front of you, sorry. I'll try to do better."

"That's OK," she said. She jumped down from her chair and ran towards me to throw her arms around me.

I looked at her legs and I looked at the techs. "You made these for her?"

"Figured she deserved them," Shifton said, "but we're all out of material now. We barely had enough to make one set of child's legs. I can't make anymore. As you can see, these are high-grade. We need raw materials."

"Excellent workmanship."

"Thank you," the tech team said in unison.

Tamara squirmed from my grip and continued to check energy cells.

"How many did you invite to this party?" I looked over the weapons and saw enough for a small militia.

"This is just for us," Shifton began, "I'm coming with you. Moth will stay here with Tamara. We're hoping Laiten can get away. All other able bodies are en route from outside the station. They haven't checked in yet. It's unsafe to

139

contact them until they're through security.

"We picked up some chatter," Mothball's pale face looked alien in the glow of the energy cell he inserted into the last weapon. "Whoever is disposing of the people in the pods is planning to move in and retrieve them. They have major clout. They've got permission to lock down Research Division while they do it."

"When?"

"That's what we don't know," he continued, "could be today, now, next week." Mothball shook his head and sighed.

"Are you going to tell me what the plan is?" I asked. "You can't just get these people out and send them back to their lives as if nothing has happened."

"Not yet. Later when it's too late for you to talk us out of it," Shifton replied.

I closed my eyes. They were resourceful. I dreaded to think what they had come up with. "Short term plan?" I asked.

"Get into the room and guard the pods until backup arrives. If we have time to wake them up, arm them and put them in a safe, defensive position, then we will. Backup will infiltrate the tunnel system your knee would struggle with, so you'll have to go back through Ethan's."

"I'm sure he won't mind," I muttered.

An alert sounded on a nearby screen. Mothball scooted his chair towards the noise. He screwed up his face. "What the hell does that mean?"

"What?" I asked.

"It's raining on Nartern Eleven."

"Oh for f… sake," I joined him while I tempered my language for Tamara's benefit.

"You know what this means?" he asked.

"Yes. No, not really. It's something I thought was private between me and Jarner. Obviously, I was mistaken."

The door opened and Laiten entered to be greeted by raised weapons.

"Sorry," I said lowering my gun.

"We're taking these," Shifton indicated three large backpacks, "basic provisions, water, something to eat."

Another alert interrupted her.

"Bring the bonus underpants, you may need them," Mothball read, "What the hell?"

"Ignore it. I think someone is trying to unnerve me." I hoisted a backpack over my shoulders and grunted at the weight. As I added an ankle gun, I almost fell onto my head as the bag's weight shifted, much to Tamara's amusement. I stuck my tongue out at her and winked.

"Second thoughts, Track, rather than the long route, can you manage a six-rung ladder on that knee?" Shifton asked.

"Does it get us there any quicker?" I asked.

"Yes. This place is a nonsense of tunnels and shafts. Moth found a quick way into Ethan's I wish I'd known about earlier." Shifton opened the doors leading to the room where Hegland's body was entombed. The gases which had enveloped Hegland's box as it entered the inner room had been disabled. I glanced in his general direction, still unsure what his part was in all this.

I felt a hand on my shoulder as Laiten encouraged me to move on.

"Take it easy you two," I called to Mothball and Tamara as we followed Shifton along the wall to a crude opening at the side.

She handed us strap-on lights for our heads. "The lights are out until we turn the corner."

I pointed to a sledgehammer sitting at the side of the hole.

"Don't need it, Moth used it to break through."

Leaving me at the top of the short ladder attached to the wall inside the tunnel I could feel their eyes on me as I made my way down. Holy nephew of Sasken, that hurt like a… forget it, there are no words. I reached the bottom red-faced, fighting tears and grateful neither Shifton nor Laiten asked if I was OK. I might have cried.

Yes, there was light at the end of the tunnel. We turned the corner and hit a dead end. Shifton leant against the wall and a portion unclipped and swung towards us.

"Have we shifted in dimension?" I asked as I recognised another section of Ethan's 'Ol Bar.

We skirted some businessmen who paid us no notice and filtered into the storage area and the door leading to Research Division.

The bright lights of Research took me by surprise. As I was adjusting to the light, we heard gunfire.

"Cover us," Shifton said as she and Laiten stepped away to tackle the door to Eight Seven Four Six. I swung my weapon around the corner and stared down the barrel of a hastily withdrawn gun to be met with the face of a dead man.

Jarner.

20

Jarner

I stepped into the main corridor, right into the line of fire
from whoever wanted the bio-pods. A combination of my
not-so-dead husband pushing, and Laiten dragging propelled
my useless carcass into Eight Seven Four Six. Someone shut
us in, away from the gunfire and yells of frustration outside.
I was aware of things going on around me, but I had no
ability to help. I remember tilting my head and staring at
Jarner as my brain tried to work out what the hell was
happening. My weapon clattered to the floor, but I hardly
heard it. I reached for Jarner and kissed him roughly before I
pulled back in a daze. Somebody, it turns out it was me,
threw a fist at Jarner's jaw knocking him off balance and
against the sealed door.

"I guess I deserved that."

"You're dead," I managed.

"About that," Jarner began.

I cut him off with some very bad words and was about to
reconnect my fist with other parts of Jarner's anatomy when
Shifton interceded. She appeared between us in her most
terrifying countenance. "Track, this will have to wait. You
need to stop them from reaching the door," she turned to
Jarner, raised a fist and cracked him on the side of the face.
"That's for putting my friend through hell," her eyes glared
disgust while she pointed to the door and yelled, "Now,
defend."

She was right. Whoever was on the other side would have
all the access codes they needed to open her up, walk right in

and take us out, if we didn't stop them. It seemed counterintuitive to open the door and fire at them, but we were out of options.

Jarner cracked the door open and fired a few shots up the corridor. Our friendly greeting was met with much the same from the other end. I took my turn, my clumsy aim ricocheted off a nearby wall as I couldn't tear my eyes from the impossible in front of me.

"Are you at least going to point that thing in the right direction," he complained.

"Are you going to tell me what the hell is going on?" I asked.

"Can we wait until fewer people are firing at us?" he swung his weapon around the door. "That's gotta hurt," he said making room in the doorway for me to see a black-clad figure with a leg wound being dragged back around the distant corner.

"I don't recognise them. They're not Authority."

"Private contractors, to put it politely."

"Why are you alive?" I asked, choosing the wrong words.

"Ah, that's such a huge question for…"

"You know what I mean, you sarcastic arsehole." My voice was so high I felt I should call on Tamara to do some talking for me and interject some adult tones.

"*I'm* a sarcastic arsehole? That's rich coming from you."

"Close the door for a minute and get over here," Laiten yelled, putting a screen on a desk. I looked around at the faces of people, some of whom I recognised from my fixing days. They ranged from people propped up in chairs being supported by more able-bodied amputees to those with three-quarters of their limbs still attached. All of them added a green hue to their normal grey tinge. A couple of people threw up as discreetly as possible. They helped each other with bottles of water as I realised my next task.

Between the four of us, we heaved the pods into a defensive wall in front of our rescued civilians. They were in no state to leave the room. "How are we getting them out of here?" I asked, "Any secret doors?"

"Not that I know of," Shifton grunted at the weight of the last pod we moved into position.

"Mickley is adding the words," Laiten said.

"Will someone please tell me what the fuck is going on. Sorry," I apologised to the young ones present and a couple of disapproving older ones.

"I filmed everyone before they were woken and after they were revived," Laiten said, "Proof of life. I uploaded the video to Mothball and Mickley is hacking the station-wide announcement system. Lax is on Authority Six relaying the story system-wide."

"You need this," Jarner said. I never thought I'd hear that voice again and for a second, I was immobilised. He produced Banyon's eye from a pocket.

"You took Banyon's eye?" I hissed.

"This isn't your Banyon's eye. I picked a few up from the obsolete bins at the back of the stores, it's just a data drive." Jarner checked the charge on his weapon before continuing, "I needed to draw Hegland out and get him on camera. He knew I'd been accumulating footage but didn't know where I was storing it. He saw me with this before I shook him off. Hours later he saw me heading home. I'd already stashed the drives somewhere else and stuck a dog-cam in the corner of the kitchen ceiling. I hoped it would pick him up if he took the bait. He attacked me and when I didn't have the drive on me, he assumed I'd put it in Banyon's head." Jarner paused to upload files to Mothball.

"Hegland ransacked our apartment?" I asked.

Jarner nodded. "I don't know why he only took one eye, he should have taken both of them to be sure. Sloppy. Neither would have done him any good."

"That door won't hold," Laiten interrupted.

"Got it," I heard Mothball's voice over the screen's speaker.

"What's on the drive?" I asked.

"Proof."

A crack in the door interrupted Jarner's explanation. A shot flew over my head as we ducked behind the pods to defend ourselves and Si-Cross Four's so-called missing Remnants.

"Why did Hegland come back to our apartment? Was it for the second eye?" I asked.

Jarner screwed his face up at me. "That was me. I swapped the dog-cam from the kitchen with the remaining eye, so you'd find it. I wasn't even sure the camera was working." He pushed his weapon above the makeshift barricade and fired at whoever was on the other side.

Recalling the details of that incident, I yelled over gunfire. "You shot at me. You could have killed me."

"You'd be dead if I wanted you dead. I was terrified you wouldn't be up to defending yourself after the decontamination if Hegland made himself known. I had to check on you."

"What were you doing in the kitchen?" I was potentially focusing on the wrong things at this point.

"I was hungry. Can we do this later? I don't think these guys will stop for us to have a full-blown domestic."

I was so enraged, I stuck my head above the barricade in full view of enemy soldiers and took out one of the nearest before realising I didn't possess a personal shield and ducked down again.

"You were dead."

"I didn't like it much. I was taken prisoner for a while. They have technology and knowledge. Mind games. I forgot... a lot," he stopped and let his gun do the talking.

"Bastards," I hissed, my anger got the better of me and I fired at, and missed an incoming monster of a man armed to the hilt. Jarner knocked me out of the way and forced the guy into a state of death with a hail of weapons fire more accurate than my own.

"Will you focus? I'd like to not die today," he reprimanded.

A battle erupted outside our room. "They're here,"

Shifton announced.

I'd given up trying to understand exactly what was going on. "You're hit," I said breaking out of my useless state and took a sterile cloth handed to me by a civilian.

"Yeah, plenty of them about in a place that fixes service bots. The rest of us can just wipe our wounds with infected rags," she said.

I tied the cloth around Shifton's upper arm.

"It barely touched me, I'm fine," she protested.

It was neither the time nor the place. "Did you know Jarner was alive?" I asked.

"No. I swear, if I had known, I wouldn't have kept that from you."

I looked from Shifton to Laiten who shook his head, said nothing and wouldn't make eye contact with me. I would always hold that suspicion. "So, what now?" I asked, "we're effectively cornered. There's no way out and the mother of all battles is going on outside," I took a deep breath and shook my head. "I don't even know who's fighting who anymore. So, what do we do?"

"We wait," Shifton replied.

A defunct screen on a nearby wall struggled to come to life. The network connected and crackled. Laiten adjusted the screen he'd been using earlier.

Video footage of the pods and the people inside appeared on the screen. In the background, I could see my weapon drop to the floor, the frenzied kiss and the punch I threw at my husband's face. Thankfully, the focus was on other people. The video jumped to a group of exhausted, dishevelled people in various stages of injury where most of them still sat.

Mickley's voice filled the void over the network. *"These civilians of Si-Cross Four, survivors of the recent Sepnid 7 outbreak had been kidnapped and put into stasis while their ill-fitting and discontinued artificial limbs were confiscated. Three civilians remain unaccounted for. As they were in greater need of care, we suspect they have been disposed of."*

My mind jumped to my old neighbour. He was there one day and then just gone, I had been too caught up in my grief for Jarner to contemplate anything insidious.

The video changed and showed a room I recognised. It was the room Laiten and I crawled past on our first trip into Research. I felt Jarner's presence at my shoulder. "You really need to keep your arse down more when you're crawling around. I'd recognise it anywhere."

"That *was* you in the room! I thought they saw us when they came out. You distracted them?"

He nodded.

"These men and women are guilty of conspiracy to kidnap, murder and create the illegal Abyss narcotic using components found inside the Si-Cross Four civilians' artificial limbs."

The video showed the faces of the people in the room, except Jarner's. I guess he'd filmed it on a hidden camera. The same group of people stood in a lab I didn't recognise watching an elaborate procedure extract the minutest amount of fluid from an artificial arm before the limb was discarded and the drop of liquid revered.

All this? For that? My jaw dropped open. "This was all about the production of Abyss? When did production start again?"

"After Sepnid 7" Jarner said, "They didn't want to spend any money. They threw a crate of artificial limbs over here from years ago. Old models, discontinued and superseded tech. Before it left the storage facility, someone found a leaking limb and had themselves quarantined until the sticky substance on his hands could be isolated and proved to be harmless. And it was. But someone in the lab realised it possessed a similar chemical structure to the missing element of synthetic Abyss. It was less than perfect, but when has perfection been necessary for drug trafficking?"

Adrenaline left my body, and I sagged towards the cold, grey metal of the nearest bio-pod in our defensive wall. "And this was what the military had you investigating during the war?" I asked.

Jarner nodded. "Several high-ranking officials made some disastrous decisions whilst under the influence of Abyss. They got me out of the hell I was held in, killed me in action, absolutely forbade me from contacting you and had me infiltrate the management undercover. Apparently, I have one of those faces that'll blend in anywhere. During the course of my investigation, I found out Hegland was an addict and working for the other side. I guess he OD'd somewhere."

Shifton joined me against the pod of exhausted souls. I tilted my head upwards and listened.

"They've stopped firing," I said and stood ready to walk to the door. She held me back with a touch on my arm. The resurrection of my husband had caused all sense to desert me.

"Until they come in declaring which side they're on, in whatever manner they choose, stay put," Shifton instructed.

"I have a question," I said with hesitation. If I didn't get the answer I was hoping for, I would have myself hospitalised. "Did you send me any messages in the last few days?" I turned my head to Jarner and waited, "via any of the system screens, or service bots?" I added.

Jarner smiled. "I picked up a few tricks while I was under," he said.

"You bast…" the door burst open.

"Stand down Track, we're on the same side."

Beynard.

I stood and gave him my best, "but you *never* leave your office" frown.

He strode further into the room and addressed our civilians. "Medical personnel will be here soon. We'll get you checked out in medical and see what we can do about replacing your limbs. We may need to ask Track to swear a lot and pay into the swear jar."

Jarner made himself visible. "Did you round them all up?" he asked.

"Yes. They were all where you said they'd be. We've got

two team members in critical condition, but they should pull through. I'm not losing any sleep over the ones we took out. The ignorance and arrogance to believe they'd stand a chance of getting away with it. Exceptional work Jarner. Thank you. It's good to have you back."

My commanding officer and my not-dead husband shook hands. A few more words were spoken, leaving me in no doubt. Beynard knew Jarner was still alive. He knew the mission, and he kept everything from me. A red mist fell over my eyes and the whooshing in my ears increased as my blood pressure soared.

"Track?" I heard Jarner but ignored him.

"Track?" I heard a long drawn out "Nooooooo!"

I lost control. There was no stopping it. I pulled back my arm. As my fist connected with Beynard's jaw it was lights out for the man who decided on my future reinstatement.

21
Epilogue

I was still off duty during the frenzied aftermath. Part of me hoped Beynard would require my presence back in uniform. Maybe he would have done if I hadn't decked him. What was I supposed to do? He knew my husband was alive and continued to let me believe I'd lost him. I'm damned sure I could have kept that a secret for the sake of the operation; I was back to being angry at everyone.

I couldn't tell if Laiten knew about Jarner or not. Consequently, there was a new distance between us. He hadn't been by with baked ants in a while and he hadn't returned my calls.

Banyon finished his game of fetch with a human hiccup for a bark. Voice modules had kept me amused, again. He still had his demon eye, and I pretended it had the ability to cut people down with a laser beam. I finished drinking my coffee and pulled my arm back ready to hurl my mug against the wall when someone rang the toilet flush sound on my doorbell. Jarner had kept his distance from me whilst finishing up the tail end of the operation; rounding up as many of the guilty he could with everyone else's help. I don't know why I was expecting Jarner to be on the other side of the door; he had a key card and biometric access to the apartment. I couldn't bring myself to revoke them when I thought he was dead.

The second toilet flush alerted me to the fact I hadn't dragged myself out of my chair to open the door. Lowering my arm, I deposited my mug and groaned as I pulled myself upright. "I'm coming," I muttered under my breath. I was about to bite someone's head off until I saw who it was. "Wicklow, come in." She'd been crying or fighting back tears. "Sit down," I gestured to a spare chair. I sat while she paced.

"I've fucked it all up, Track. It's all a fucking mess." She landed heavily in a chair, dropped her head into her hands and cried.

I toyed with the idea of going over to her and offering comfort. In the end, it took me a few seconds to realise she'd stopped crying and was getting a grip on her emotions, while I was wondering what to do. I sat, and I waited.

She stared at me with red-rimmed eyes. "I'm pregnant."

"I know. You told me before the decontamination process, remember?" I asked. I'll admit, in all the mayhem of the last few weeks, Wicklow's pregnancy had slipped my mind. She wasn't showing yet, but even so, some friend I was.

"I forgot I told you," her voice was barely audible. She took a shuddering breath. I minimised my groaning as I pulled myself out of the chair to get her some water from the kitchen. She stared at it on the table before continuing. "I just found out what happened to Hegland and what part he played in all this."

My brain did a double take before jumping to conclusions. We were talking about Wicklow's pregnancy and now Hegland. The last time I had seen my partner alive, he'd been having a heated discussion with Wicklow. I groaned. If what I suspected was true, Wicklow had indeed fucked up.

"You were having an affair with Hegland, and the baby is his."

More tears ran down her cheek to accompany the quiet sobbing and her nodding head.

"And your husband?"

"Gone. As soon as I told him I was pregnant, he knew it wasn't his. He had tests done and knew he couldn't have children. Not that he bothered to tell me."

We could hear raised voices from my neighbours. So much for them complaining about Banyon's bark.

"What am I going to do?" she asked.

I was too tired to be anything other than blunt. "Well, you can't do any more undercover work that takes you away from your child for weeks at a time. Your baby needs a parent. You'll have to commit to Si-Cross Four business only and use the childcare we have on offer. You should be able to support two of you on an Authority payment schedule." I suppose I could have gone with *don't worry, it'll be OK.* She nodded her head. I silently patted myself on the back for saying, if not the right thing, then at least something that wasn't appalling.

"Thank you. Most of my friends are Bart's family. You can imagine the reception I've had from them. Nothing like bringing another man's child into the world to alienate your in-laws."

"Oh, that's bull. Most of your friends are in Authority Four. We look after our own. We do it with scraps of food and bits of frayed string, but we do what we can."

The voices from next door raised once more and something fragile shattered on the other side of my wall.

Before I could say anything, Wicklow jumped to her feet and yanked my door open, hissing, "That's it, I have had enough." Her short fuse had just burnt out.

I followed and caught up with her as Wicklow was pounding on my neighbour's door demanding entry to the apartment on Authority business.

The woman answered, I'd forgotten her name. Wicklow pushed past the woman. I followed before she could slam the door in my face. While Wicklow was regaining her composure, I looked around the apartment. It had the same layout as mine and I'd been here many times before, visiting the old man before this couple moved in.

"Where's your husband?" I asked the woman. She looked at me like someone had smeared her upper lip with excrement. She lunged at Wicklow who was in no mood to be messed with and pulled her weapon, stunning the woman to the ground.

"To the point," I muttered, "keep her here, I'll look for the husband."

He wasn't hard to find. I followed the moans and groans and found him sprawled on the bedroom floor, bleeding with one arm at an awkward angle. I checked his body, his shirt was open showing a torso full of bruises at various stages of healing. You just don't know what goes on behind closed doors. I'd have had the guy pegged as the one capable of abuse if I'd had to guess. Now? Now I was running on the assumption he was overcompensating for an abusive wife when the woman died at my door a zillion years ago. Cries for help needed to be more obvious and come with flashing lights.

I used the *don't worry, it's going to be OK* line and joined Wicklow in the living room. The woman was awake and hissed at me. I gave her a suitable "grow up woman" look and pulled my weapon from my belt.

"Cuff her. Call it in while I keep her under control. This is domestic violence and her husband needs medical attention." Authority business kept Wicklow's mind off her personal troubles for a while.

***

When the loving wife next door had been dealt with and the husband whisked away for treatment, I tidied a corner of my workshop. My hand recoiled from the tube Shifton had me retrieve from Research Division like it was radioactive or covered in acid. I reached for the desk comms before remembering my internal hotline and tapped my neck. "Shif…ton where are you?" I sang.

She connected and launched into a conversation as if we'd been talking for hours.

"There was nothing on that other hidden file in Banyon's eye. We're still looking, but it seems to be empty. I've got the results," she said.

"Of?"

"The lubricant bottle you handed in."

After a few seconds of silence, I remembered the one I'd swapped from the civilian at my last fixing day. I'd been so distracted by the pain in my knee and the accompanying fatigue, I had forgotten I'd handed it over. Being kept out of the loop for a couple of weeks, I had lost all ability to function.

"The new lubricant the civilians were issued for their prosthetics."

"Right, I remember," I said as my brain caught up.

"We're rounding up all the bottles and confiscating them."

"Because?"

"Because it's toxic, Track. Where have you been?... Sorry, I forgot they're still keeping you in the dark. Well, sod protocol. This stuff is a long-term toxin. It won't do any harm in the short-term, but in the long-term, repeated exposure to the skin can cause life-threatening illnesses."

"Was it supplied with intent to harm or were they just fucking ignorant?"

"I'd like to think the latter, but I have a feeling it was part of their plan. It just didn't work quick enough."

"Have you got all the bottles?" I asked.

"Think so."

"Have they rounded up all the people involved in the conspiracy?" I thought I'd ask, seeing as Shif was in a chatty mood. This was more information than I'd been given in the last two weeks.

"All but two. There are always two who manage to slip through the net. This is me you're talking to, call them what you like."

"Fucking arseholes."

"Well, as far as rants go, that was pathetic."

"Thank you." I changed the subject, "I've still got your tube of nuclear waste here."

"Huh?"

"The container of deadly poison you had me pocket from Research."

"Oh, Rosie's skin. Excellent. Can you drop it by when you get a chance? Bring Banyon. There should be enough to make him a spare fur too."

I held up the tube to eye-level and wondered how a hand-length, thin container would be enough to cover an ear let alone an entire capybara and a dog.

It was, would you believe, another Tuesday when I was summoned to Beynard's lair.

"Track, sit," Beynard ordered.

"Woof," I disguised my bark as an exhalation of relief as I slumped into the seat. Again, I found their familiar discomfort, comforting. It's funny what you get used to and what you miss when it's taken away from you.

The door opened behind me. "Good, Jarner, please, take a seat," Beynard said with respect and without barking it as an order. I tried not to glare.

I glanced at my husband, the state of our relationship was unknown. We'd hardly seen each other since his resurrection.

I'd refused to guess why I'd been summoned. Now I was present, thoughts attacked my brain. I had decked my commanding officer. I'd gone rogue in an unsanctioned operation. Or, at least, my part was unsanctioned… Actually, I had no bloody idea what was going on. I was probably about to be fired permanently and Jarner was there to prevent me from ending Beynard.

"You did good work, Track. Although why you took so long to get down to Mickley at the COC, I'll never know."

"I was kidnapped and dragged there," I complained.

Beynard shrugged. "You weren't following my instructions. I told you to check out the COC, you didn't. You can take the rest of the week, then I'll expect you back at your desk on Monday.

I am not an unintelligent man. I am also not slow on the uptake. But this? This threw me. I don't know what my husband and Beynard discussed while I was piecing together the whole thing. I'd been sent undercover after being suspended whilst not being suspended. What the… my voice faltered, "Why didn't you just put me undercover? Why go through this whole rigmarole of suspending me? And why the hell not just come out with instructions of going to the COC rather than suggesting I take up Swayleum Knitting or whatever they were doing that week?"

Beynard lent forward on his desk, interrupting his conversation with Jarner. "Track, no-one in his right mind would send you, of all people, to the COC. Have you seen the courses available down there? I thought you'd see right through it." He turned to look at my husband. "Maybe we should have brought him in on the entire plan."

Jarner shook his head. "Too dangerous."

I saw red and shouted in my defence. "I'm not that much of a liability undercover…" I stopped shouting. The words wouldn't sound through Jarner's hand covering my mouth. I licked it. He hated that.

"When I was captured," Jarner wiped his hand on his trouser leg in disgust, "they threatened your life. You had to be suspended, they couldn't know you were still on the job, they were too close. Did you ever feel someone was following you?" he asked. I nodded. "It wasn't always me. If they thought you were in on it, they'd take you to get to me. I couldn't let that happen. I've seen what they do to people. I had a network of insiders ready to help out if you got stuck in Research or needed access through doors, but none of them had combat skills."

I thought back to the people Laiten and I met in Research and the man who opened a door for us. There was another who distracted the group of people who otherwise would have seen us down there. I assumed they were all in on it. It would have been nice to know at the time.

"Moving on to other business," Beynard began and just like that, my rights to any further knowledge of the inner workings of our exploits were glossed over.

"The Authority seized the assets of the main players," Beynard looked thrilled with himself. "The wealth they have confiscated is vast."

"Fantastic," I began, "and what is Authority Six laying claim to now?" I asked of one of our bigger and better places.

"Nothing. This was an Authority Four operation and we reap the rewards. Research Division is no longer a secret. They are openly working on replacement limbs for our survivors. They won't be state-of-the-art, but they'll be far superior to any they've used before. You're back on the list for a knee replacement. But, Track, you hit a commanding officer, I can't push you to the top of the list. You'll have to wait."

I was relieved I was being considered for treatment at all, waiting would not be a problem.

"Will all the survivors be treated equally?" I asked.

"Yes. You'll see to that. Check your messages, there are links to manufacture and maintenance procedures. Co-ordinate with Mickley at the COC."

My head turned slowly, and my wide eyes told him he'd better not be buggering about.

***

Back in our apartment, I walked into the kitchen three times before I remembered what I was there for and brewed coffee. How could I forget coffee?

"Have you sorted it all out yet?" Jarner asked. He was still physically keeping his distance, wisely so.

"What do you mean?" I asked.

"I know you, people bombard you with information. You say nothing about it until you've mulled it over and compartmentalised it. Is it all in the right boxes yet?"

"Is that what I do?" I wasn't mad at him. I was in too much pain and too tired for that.

"Don't be too hard on Laiten. I needed someone with you I could trust. I owe him more than he'll ever owe me," he paused. "You had figured out he knew I was alive?"

"I wasn't sure until now. Was there anyone else kept in the dark, or was it just me?"

"The only people who knew were Beynard and Laiten. Laiten is one of the good guys. He saved my life. He pushed me away from the acid spray and nearly lost his sight. I can't imagine how long it took to get used to seeing a different face in the mirror every day."

Jarner read my look perfectly. I had no idea. I knew about Laiten's acid attack, but not that Laiten had saved Jarner in the process. Dropping my head back, I stared at the ceiling before closing my eyes and letting out another long sigh.

"You're a decorated war hero," I began, "how did these sub-human bastards not know it was you?"

"You think these people look any further than their own sad little lives? They're so far up their own orifices they only see their supply of narcotics, plush surroundings and financial figures. I doubt they'd paid attention to news reports covering wider issues."

I smiled at that, we were similar in a lot of ways.

Something hit me in the chest and dropped to the floor. I looked down and picked up the scrap of gold material I'd been offered in the clothing outlet.

"You left them behind. It took a lot of effort to hack all the systems, you could at least have taken your bonus underpants."

"Happy to watch you try them on." I pounced as Jarner's jaw dropped and stuffed the gold material into his open mouth.

"I have things to do before I go back to work on Monday."

"You're not going," he said spitting out the offending garment. "While you zoned out in Beynard's office, I informed him we were having some time off together. You'll have plenty of time to read up about limb maintenance. The new ones shouldn't need much ongoing work. I've got a trip planned."

"Yeah? Where to?" I wandered back into the living room

with my coffee and stopped to straighten a cushion on a chair.

"Track, do you remember Nartern Eleven?"

The cushion hit Jarner square in the face.

About the Author

Living and working in South East England, DJ Cooper is an author of science fiction with a flair for humour and the bizarre. A wife, mother and business owner, she splits her time between many things, rarely completing anything. You can follow her at

https://djsworld.co.uk/

and

https://medium.com/@debzcooper

where random thoughts are regularly unleashed onto an unsuspecting public.

Other social media platforms are updated on a hit and miss basis and probably not worth bothering with. However, for completeness, here is a list:

Twit-thing:

https://twitter.com/BarkingMadDJ

Face-thing:

https://www.facebook.com/DJCooperFiction/

Read-thing:

https://www.goodreads.com/author/show/173857 92.D_J_Cooper

That-picture-thing:

https://www.instagram.com/barkingmaddj/

Also by DJ Cooper

The Illusion
Book 2 of A Bulwark Anthology